LLOY

EDEN'S WAR

FOREWORD

IN THE FIRST OF THIS series – "A Distant Eden" - Adrian Hunter was orphaned at an early age and raised by his uncle Roman and aunt Sarah. On graduation from high school he joined the army. His large size and athletic build, along with a keen sense of duty and abnormally high IQ caused him to be quickly recruited into special operations. Several years into his military career, while stationed at Fort Hood, a huge coronal mass ejection from the sun wiped out the world's electric grids.

The army, being unable to feed its soldiers, discharged the vast majority of the military. Left to make it on his own Adrian and several of his fellow team-mates walked to Fort Brazos (as it was to become known) where Roman lived. Roman was a prepper, had been most of his life, and had created a survivable environment. Roman was exceedingly glad to have Roman and his troops on board. After many adventures and a war with a neighboring but hostile faction, Adrian settled down at Fort Brazos and married.

In the second book of the series - "Adrian's War" - his wife, a doctor, soon died from a plague disease from a patient she treated. Adrian, heartbroken, set off on his own on a journey. He'd believed that by moving to the Rocky Mountains he could live a life of solitude. But as soon as he arrived he became embroiled in a war with a group of cannibalistic raiders.

In the third book - "Eden's Hammer" - Adrian returned to Fort Brazos after a call for help from Roman. A large band of vicious raiders were heading directly for Fort Brazos and Adrian created a militia, trained them, and took on the raiders. He became involved in not just a war with the raiders, but a personal war as well.

The fourth book – "Eden's Warriors" – describe a situation that Adrian gets into that propels him into a leadership role he never wanted, but performed out of a sense of duty. Adrian was forced to grow in ways he never dreamed of.

This fifth book is a culmination of the series. Adrian is thrust into an even larger role, again one he doesn't want, but is duty bound to carry out. He reluctantly grows into the role, and takes on a responsibility larger than any he had ever, even in his worst nightmares, thought he would have to take on.

DEDICATION

THIS BOOK IS DEDICATED TO my family and the many loyal fans of this series. To my wonderful wife, my children, my brother and sisters and nephews and nieces. If it wasn't for their constant encouragement it would never have been written.

I have also been blessed to receive a continual stream of encouraging emails and reviews, those readers too helped write this book, in more ways than I can enumerate. Thank you to each and every one of you.

CHAPTER 1

RACE GENTLY SQUEEZED THE TRIGGER. She was too focused to feel the slight recoil as the .223 bullet left the barrel at three-thousand-five-hundred feet per second. She didn't hear the loud roar of the expanding gases leaving the barrel behind the bullet either. She was too intently focused on her target, a portion of the man's head protruding from behind a tree limb, for sensations to register. Her eyes were locked on the front sight and the man's head, the back sight more of a blur.

As the hot gasses exited the barrel there was a micro-second of heat bloom that distorted her vision of the target, but the distortion disappeared immediately and she saw the red mist that blossomed behind the man as the bullet entered, expanded, and exited the back of his head, blowing out bone, brain tissue, and blood in a spray of fine particles.

One down, three to go.

She had tracked the four men for two days. A Texas Ranger, Race and her wolf, Bear, were at the end of a six-week rotation of solo patrols, and had been on their way home for a much-needed rest when their path crossed the raiders' trail.

The newly re-established Texas Rangers were not much like their original's name sake. Or maybe they were but only in the original Ranger's earliest days. The new Republic of Texas was in desperate need of law and order, but it also needed to make a fast and decisive cut into the number of criminals roaming the countryside at will. The new republic was still woefully short of formal law proceedings.

The new Rangers – unofficially called Race's Rangers where the female Rangers were concerned – operated in several different modes. There were solo excursions such as Race was currently on, "Patrols" or trio-teams, where three Rangers worked together, and occasionally full size "Companies" of ten. Periodically the Rangers would team up with a local militia when the size of the operation required it.

Race had been heading back to Fort Brazos when Bear suddenly took off in a different direction. A full-grown, adult wolf, raised and trained by Race's adoptive father, Adrian, Bear weighed almost one-hundred pounds of sleek muscle and tough sinew. He enjoyed the hunt, and accompanied Race wherever she went.

Knowing Bear's keen senses, Race followed and soon came across two bodies – a man and woman in the front yard of a small ranch. The house had been ransacked, and a clear trail of hoof prints led away from the property. One of the disadvantages of traveling by horse was that they left easily-seen prints, not that Bear would have had any trouble finding them anyway.

Adrian had explained to the first Ranger graduating class that formal law and order could come only after the bad guys were cut down to a manageable size. At present there were far too many outlaws to try to bring them into the few courts for trial; at present imposing law and order was not a police action but a war. Thus each Ranger would be judge, jury, and executioner in the interim. "Because of this" he explained "It is imperative that you take all possible precautions to be sure of your verdict before passing and executing sentence." Race had no problem judging these four men on the evidence she had found, and she was more than sure of their guilt based on that evidence. Now she was executing the sentence.

This wasn't her first "trial" on this trip. Hopefully, it would be the last before she got home to rest. Living under the stars might sound romantic, but in practice, she had learned, it was grueling and exhausting.

She had followed the men and caught up to them in their night camp. Hobbling her own horse a sufficient distance from the camp to avoid discovery, she and Bear scouted the area and then chose her location carefully. She had a clear field of fire, while having some large rocks for cover from return fire. The men were in a mostly open area that didn't afford them much cover, and if they ran she could easily pick them off before they could get out of range. She chose her first target because he was already behind cover – although he had no idea of her presence, he just happened to be leaning against the off-side of a tree while relieving himself. The other three men were still in their bedrolls, the sun barely up. After the first shot, she calmly traversed the rifle sight to the second man and fired, then the third. The first man hadn't had time to react, the third sat up rapidly but wasn't clear on what was happening, and after she pulled the trigger he never would. The fourth man leapt to his feet and ran for the tree where she had shot the first man. An easy shot, he didn't make it halfway.

Race rode into Fort Brazos three days later, leading the four recovered horses, Bear surging out in front. She was exhausted, filthy, and dreaming of a hot bath, a hot meal and a soft bed, in that order. The sentry had sent a runner to alert Adrian of Race's approach, and Adrian was waiting for her at the barricade. Bear ran up to Adrian and powered into him at full speed. Adrian, barley rocked back by the one-hundred pound wolf missile, gathered him up in his arms and held him as easily as a baby.

Race slid out of the saddle and scratched at her matted hair. "Appears Bear missed you, he must be tired of my company."

"You look like hell." Adrian said with a grin.

"Yeah, well... I look better than the killers I found." She scratched at her hair some more, "Do you want a report right now?" The expression on her face said that she would prefer to let that wait.

"Nope, just wanted to welcome you back, and see my dog." Adrian put Bear down and stepped forward and gave Race a hard hug. She nearly disappeared in his embrace; Adrian was a huge man, easily filling a doorway with his six-foot-four inch two-hundred-eighty-pound muscular bulk. "Damn Race, you been rolling around in dead animals or something? You smell like shit. Let's get to the house, Linda's running a hot bath for you. Said it'd be the first thing you'd want. It's damn sure the first thing you *need*." He said with a big smile that took the sting off the words.

Race melted into the hug and returned it just as hard. She was happy to be home. She loved Adrian like a father, and had adopted him as one. "You married a damn smart woman General Bear. That's exactly what I want right now," she said, using the nickname Adrian had been given by the settlers because he'd once killed a huge grizzly bear with a flint-tipped spear. The settlers had later added the title of General after Adrian led them in several battles against raiders.

"How about dinner after you get cleaned up? I think we can rustle something up. Then off to the guest room for a good long sleep and you can make your report tomorrow, unless there's something urgent." Adrian turned to the sentry and said "I'll send someone for the horses."

"Nothing urgent, just the usual." Race said, fatigue in her voice.

Adrian walked her back to his and Linda's home, the large log house that the citizens of Fort Brazos had built for them after the battle of Del Rio – a large home suitable for the President of the newly formed Republic of Texas and First Lady. Bear had already gone to the house, racing ahead of them.

Linda met them at the door. Sarah greeted her far more gently than he had Adrian. She took one long, smiling look at Race, eyeing her from feet to matted hair, noticing the heavily stained clothing and overall look of exhaustion. "I'm so happy you're back healthy and safe! The bath is ready, just go straight in. I'll bring fresh clothes in a few minutes. Soak as long as you want to. Then when you're done soaking take a long hot shower – the solar tank is full and the water is nearly scalding hot."

Race gave a charmingly bright smile back to Linda, not missing the fact that Linda hadn't told her she looked like hell and smelled like shit like Adrian had. Linda's manners were always impeccable. Race noticed that Linda didn't move to give her a hug though. *Smart woman*, Race thought with an inner smile.

"Linda, you are grace personified." Race replied, then happily headed for the bathroom.

She entered the large bathroom, took her rifle off her shoulder, and stood it in a corner. Unlike its owner, the rifle was extremely clean. She next unbuckled the belt that held her knife and pistol and looped it over a towel rack, then sat on the edge of the tub and removed her boots. Following Adrian's training she had washed her feet and changed socks at least every day and sometimes more. Her feet were the cleanest part of her body at the moment. It was the most basic and fundamental training he had given her, taking care of her feet so that they didn't get into a condition that would cripple her in the field. *Good old infantry basics.* She had seen examples of how important that advice was.

Race removed the stiff and grimy camouflage fatigues, tossing them into a pile near the door. *Too far gone to wash, almost stiff enough to stand on their own*. Her clothes were stained with every kind of matter imaginable, including blood. *Probably where that dead animal smell came from.* Race removed her undergarments and looked down at the slim muscular build of an eighteen-year-old athlete. The only imperfection were the scars.

As Race stretched out in the hot soapy water a heartfelt sigh escaped her lips. *Bliss, pure and absolute bliss.*

There was a quiet knock on the door, and then Linda entered, exchanging fresh clothes for Race's soiled ones. She smiled at Race. "Doesn't get any better than that does it?"

Race just nodded in agreement and closed her eyes as Linda left the room.

She lay in the hot water, not moving, just enjoying. She thought back to the days when she was a young girl and a hot bath didn't seem at all special, back before she was thirteen, when the huge solar storm blasted the earth with a coronal mass ejection, the likes of which hadn't been seen since 1859, and probably not even then. The monster had fried the power grids in every advanced country on the planet. Starvation and disease had killed off most of the human population over a period of months following the grid dropping. By the time she was fourteen her family was dead, and she was only a few days away from dying of starvation herself when she was taken prisoner and forced into prostitution. She had endured that for three horrible years until the very happy day Adrian had rescued her and fifteen other girls from the predators that held them as slaves.

Lying in the luxury of the hot soapy water Race recalled when she first saw Adrian, dropping off Lila and Rita – two young girls he had rescued from kidnappers just a few days before, believing that the establishment was an orphanage for girls. Race smiled as she recalled trying to warn Adrian with eye signals and facial gestures not to leave the girls there, trying to signal him without her captors seeing her do it. Later Adrian told her that at first he thought she wasn't right in the head. But he had become suspicious enough to return that night and had seen what was really going on. He killed the slavers, then took all of the girls away from that awful place. She had torched it when they left.

She smiled broadly as she recalled Adrian's consternation at realizing he had saddled himself with, and had become responsible for, sixteen young girls. Adrian didn't have a clue what to do with a group of girls, so he ended up doing exactly what he would have done if they had been boys. He spent several weeks training the girls to live off the land, and in basic combat techniques. Over time he turned them into a self-sufficient and lethal team. It was his only way of giving them independence, of teaching them how to survive in this new harsh world. How to stop being victims.

It had worked far better than he had anticipated. The girls, used to being treated harshly by adults, especially men, adopted Adrian as their father, to his gradual but eventual delight. It took Adrian a long time to get used to the idea. He was a trained killer, had been a soldier in the army, had been sent on scores of special operations missions. Being a father figure to a group of young girls was a challenge he had never dreamed of facing – one he found daunting, even scary at times.

After the battle of Del Rio and becoming the President of the new Republic of Texas – another position he didn't want – Adrian created a military style academy at Fort Brazos for orphans, and installed the girls as its first class.

He re-established the Texas Rangers, and the students that graduated from the military-style academy could automatically join the Rangers, if they chose to. Race and most of the girls that Adrian rescued chose to. All of the orphan boys that found their way to the academy joined without exception. At first Adrian had intended that the school's graduates wait until the age of twenty-one to become Rangers; but in this post-grid world children had to mature faster than they had in the pre solar storm civilized world.

Within a short time Adrian relented and allowed Race to join at the age of eighteen, mostly because Race was far more mature than her years would indicate, and because she harassed him constantly on the subject. *Where in the world would I have been without Adrian? Still a slave or even more likely – dead – that's where.*

As Race put on the fresh clothes she worried about Adrian. He had been drafted into becoming the President of the Republic of Texas even though he didn't want the job, and over the past year it had been apparent he still didn't want it – but was doing it in spite of his reluctance. It had also become apparent that Adrian had become the de-facto President of the former United States, such as they were these days, and that a looming threat from across the ocean was weighing heavily on his mind.

Because Texas had the only regulated democratic government in the former USA, the military looked to him as its civilian Commander in Chief. He wasn't quick to smile anymore, and was often lost in long silences of deep thought, eyes open but not seeing his surroundings. Race could only wonder at what he *was* seeing.

This burden weighs heavily on his shoulders; broad as they are, it must be incredibly heavy all the same.

CHAPTER 2

RACE WALKED INTO LINDA'S KITCHEN. It was a large room, and the most-often used room in the house. There were two lights, powered by solar panels and batteries the village had scrounged from somewhere. A nearby spring, pipe, and gravity provided the sink with running water, a rarity these days. An old-style wood burning cook stove had also been installed. Sitting around the large table, Race saw Adrian, Linda, Adrian's uncle Roman and aunt Sarah, and the Admiral. Their conversation stopped as Race entered.

Linda quickly stood, "Race, you're just in time; sit down while I get you a cup of tea and a sandwich. We'll have a hot meal in a bit."

Adrian said, "Continue Admiral. Race obviously has our full trust and confidence."

"Of course." The Admiral was the highest ranking military officer in what was left of the former USA military, the man that had maneuvered Adrian into becoming the CIC, and involved Adrian in the war with Mexico. "The state of the former United States Military can be summed up simply as... dismal. Almost every landlocked military installation went through the same decline and abandonment as Fort Hood. After the power stopped they ran out of food and discharged over ninety-percent of their personnel so they could try to make it on their own. The few who remained eventually died of starvation or disease or just wandered off. Coastal based military fared a little better, having the ability to get food from the ocean. Still they are down to only about fifteen percent. Missile facilities have been maintained at full force though. We've taken special care to keep those troops on the job and fed." The Admiral shifted in his chair and took a sip of tea. He had, as the surviving senior military leader, found himself trying to keep a steadily deteriorating military in some semblance of order.

"Special care is being taken to provide food for the troops at the nuclear weapon sites, such as missile systems and at Pantex. Keeping those sites at one-hundred percent has been extraordinarily difficult, but per your orders we have continued to do so. The Navy and Marines are in the best shape of all, but that's only by comparison. While we have maintained forty-percent of our sailors and Marines, our fleet is only thirty percent operational, or slightly less. And those ships are not fully operational. Without satellites we are functionally down to radio and radar. The ships are coming apart little by little every day. Maintenance is severely hampered by a shortage of repair parts, no dry dock facilities, no repair infrastructure. We have located and scavenged every warehouse we know of for parts and munitions, but obviously new repair components and munitions are no longer being manufactured.

"Aircraft are in far worse shape. They take an incredible amount of daily maintenance and even a single parts failure can ground them permanently. Cannibalizing parts from grounded aircraft has reached the point of diminishing returns. Within two years we won't be able to fly anything at all, and there's not much we can fly now. Nuclear rods are no longer made, and they eventually wear out. Within four years we will be down to a small fleet of diesel-powered ships. Without a manufacturing base for repairs and re-supply we are grinding to a halt. We use our aircraft and ships only for imperative functions, giving us extra months perhaps." He took another sip of tea, then looked at Adrian with intensity.

Slowly he continued, "It sounds far-fetched... but in ten- to-fifteen years we may be looking at sailing ships again, as that will be about the only technology that a slowly emerging industrial base can handle. On top of that, we are ever more likely to get into a major confrontation with China any day now. That's why I am questioning your continued use of aircraft for these political forays you've ordered." The Admiral was uncomfortable questioning orders from the Commander In Chief, but felt it was his duty given the diminishing air-craft availability.

Adrian set his cup down carefully, paused for a long moment and then replied, "I understand all of that Admiral. With no electricity we have no manufacturing. We can't manufacture a simple wooden pencil anymore, much less the kind of manufacturing required for high-tech military applications. In plain words, where we once had over three-hundred-million people and a thriving high technology industrial base, we now have about ten-million people that were plunged in one day back into a civilization barely above stone-age technology... living for the most part off the salvage of what we once had."

Adrian stood and began pacing the kitchen while talking; he always found it difficult to be still. The rest of the group watched and listened; they were used to his barely contained energy.

"We have limited ability to continue to use some of that salvage, and to repair it on an on-going basis... and it's a rapidly downward spiral. We're not going to see a return to anything remotely like we once had within our lifetimes. We *are* going to see the end of our ability to use what little we can use now. It will be generations before we return to a technological society. If ever. Unless we can get this country organized, create an environment that allows for rapid recovery."

Adrian picked up his cup and went to the wood stove and poured himself another cup of tea. He held the pot up, a non-verbal question asking if anyone wanted a refill. The Admiral nodded and so did Race. Adrian filled their cups, returned the pot to the stove and sat back down.

"The thing about machines is they break down in storage almost as fast as they do when in use. Gaskets and O-rings get old and crack, electrical connections corrode, tires get stiff and brittle, corrosion runs rampant. Entropy doesn't stop just because you store something. We have a limited window of opportunity to use these machines. So, the question becomes, what use we can put them to during this limited time... use that is to our maximum advantage. Using them to try to recover our previous technological abilities isn't practical and neither is saving them for a future confrontation; although that is a major temptation.

"The United States of America no longer exists, and never will again. But something will. Something will take its place. We can either try to plan and direct that replacement, or we can do nothing and see what happens."

Adrian was up and pacing again. "Waiting to see what happens is a total crap-shoot. Given the history of mankind, odds are that nothing good will come of waiting. If we aren't smart... and lucky... the Chinese will take us over to serve their own purposes. They are generations ahead of us in returning to where we were. If we are going to have at it with China, then we need to organize – and we need to do it damn fast."

Adrian sat and shifted his chair forward a bit placing his arms on the table. He stared down at the wooden table top for a moment, then looking up again he said, "There are major stumbling blocks to reorganizing, and speed of travel is one of them. But it's one we can still do something about, because we still have some operational aircraft available. Sending our people to the other former states to help them organize and join together in a coalition is the best use of what we have, while we have it. A unified America will meet the Chinese threat far better than the current situation. A unified America with a society based on law and order, one that encourages entrepreneurs, one that encourages commerce, is also the best hope for our future generations to pull themselves out of the crude salvage civilization we've become and build a better and more solid future. The plan I've come up with, the one I am working hard at, will create a new kind of government, one that will best see to our children's and grandchildren's future."

Adrian paused, then with a rueful smile said, "Good Lord, I sound just like a damn politician don't I?"

Adrian stood and stretched. "Gentlemen, let's take a break. I want to hear Race's report and then she can eat a hot meal and settle down to relax a few days." He gestured to Race to follow him, "Race, let's go."

They walked along the Fort Brazos barricade, defensive fortifications that would make it a dear effort to try and take the village by force. The day was clear and mild. The pleasant smell of wood smoke from village homes was in the air. Bear walked ahead of them.

"Not much to report Adrian," said Race. "I traveled from here to Hillsboro, then on to Corsicana, down to Tehuacana, across to Mexia, then back home by way of Waco. I found and settled six individual raiders, and on the way back, near Chalk Bluff four more. Those four had killed a married couple and stolen the horses from their ranch. Didn't take long to catch up to them. Brought the horses in with me, rare things that they are. At times I think half the population turned into criminals when the grid dropped."

Adrian paused alongside one of the black-powder cannons that Matt had made. Made of heavy steel pipe, they were loaded with short pieces of chain saw blade and had demonstrated their deadly efficiency in battle. Resting his hand on the barrel he said, "About half is probably close, assuming some take to crime only when opportunity presents itself. Criminals were better suited to survive the starvation than law abiding folks were. They didn't hesitate to take what they wanted, so they lasted longer. We're making inroads into their numbers, though, and the word is getting out and dissuading some of them from continuing to raid productive people, or to think twice when opportunity arises. In time we'll get them down to a manageable number, but it's going to take a couple of years at least."

They started walking back to the house and Race said, "I hadn't thought much about how we're going to build our country back up. Hearing you talk about losing what technology we've been able to salvage was depressing. Don't you think maybe we can get back faster than that?"

"Well...I'd love to be wrong...but I just don't see it. There are a lot of similarities between war strategy and politics. More than I would have believed a year ago. I've come to believe that the most important part of what a government provides its people is a safe, law-abiding, environment. A place where individuals can put their efforts into having new ideas and creating things, instead of putting their efforts into fighting off bad guys for every ear of corn they grow. You and the rest of the Rangers are instrumental in that goal. Pushing back the raiders gives the farmers and ranchers the time, and room, to work on expanding. Expanding their operations means more food. More food means there's more time for some young genius to educate himself, and then to invent something that he can manufacture, and sell to others. It has a snowball effect, each person whose life is touched by that genius's idea or thing has a chance of sparking another new idea, or they figure out how to improve on it."

As they reached the house again Adrian stopped Race at the door. "You're living a dangerous life, Race. A hard life that is exhausting and brutal. But what you do has a direct impact on how fast and how far we can go in this new world we live in. You are doing good work, helping all of us. Remember that on the days that you judge and execute the criminals that are holding us back. I'm proud of you Race, as proud as I can be." Adrian gave her a long hug. "Thank you for what you are doing. Thank you from the bottom of my heart."

As they entered the house Adrian turned for the kitchen, but Linda waved Race over into the living room. "I've put a hot meal for you in the study, looks like the Admiral has a lot more to talk about and I thought you might want to eat and then get some sleep."

"Great idea Linda... and thank you." Race said.

Linda watched Race walk into the study. "Looks like Adrian has done it again, that girl is glowing," she said aloud, though no one was listening. "He hates being a politician, but he damn sure knows how to inspire and lead people."

"Adrian." The general said calling out from the kitchen. "We've got new intelligence on China, and you need to hear it."

CHAPTER 3

ADRIAN STUDIED THE ADMIRAL'S FACE. He'd only known him for a year, but it had been a long year that included a war with former drug cartels from Mexico. It felt like they'd known each other a lot longer than they had. They had grown close in that year, with the Admiral being the closest thing to a mentor that Adrian had known in a long time. It was the Admiral who had cornered Adrian into becoming the civilian Command in Chief because as President of the Republic of Texas he was the only acknowledged leader of anything in what had once been the United States.

Adrian could see the tightening of the crow's feet around the Admiral's grey eyes, noted the lowered pitch of voice; signals to Adrian that the news wasn't good. He knew the Admiral well enough to spot signs of tension, a here was a lot of tension.

"Sit down and tell me," said Adrian

They sat, accepting the cups of rare coffee Sarah brought them She had bartered heavily to get a small amount of the beans. She smiled at the Admiral, then left the room to check on Race.

The Admiral played with his coffee cup for a moment, swirling the black liquid around. "Adrian, the intelligence reports we have are sketchy at best.

We have two submarines patrolling off the Chinese coast that pick up occasional radio traffic and what they can see by radar and periscope. Most of that traffic we can't decipher, so we don't have much that's of military origin. We catch an occasional bit of commercial talk though. Putting together what we have, we think they are going to be coming a lot sooner than we had originally thought. The bad news is they could begin moving in three months, maybe less."

Adrian looked at his hands for a moment, not noticing the scars, not noticing his hands at all. "And the good news?" he asked.

"None," replied the admiral tiredly. "No good news of any kind."

"What's their latest ship count?"

"Their naval ships have all been put back into action. Their surface ships about match ours in number, but not in capability. In an open battle we would win. They have eleven nuclear subs, those worry me some. They've been frantically collecting and refurbishing every large commercial vessel they can find and tow back to their harbors. Fishing boats, cruise ships, container ships, and tankers. Our best count right now is somewhere in the neighborhood of fifteen-hundred of those. Those worry me a lot. With their almost unlimited resource of personnel, they can man every one of those ships and easily put over a million total fighting men on them. Some of those men would be new recruits – forced recruits probably – but with two months of training, that is still going to be a major force to contend with. An all-out assault, using all the ships, coming at the west coast simultaneously, in spread out formation... and protected by their war ships..." the Admiral shook his head. "It could be insurmountable using conventional warfare. We could be looking at the necessity of using nukes to take out large chunks of their fleet at a time."

"And if they come at us spread as far apart as they can, how effective will our nukes be?" Adrian asked. "Wouldn't it be more effective to nuke their harbors right now to take out not only their ships but also their shipworks?"

The Admiral took a sip of his coffee without answering. He understood a rhetorical question when he heard one.

After a long silence, Adrian said "We can knock them out where they are right now. We have the capacity for that."

The Admiral answered, "Yes. We can damage them to the point that they won't be able to attack and shove them back years in their efforts, bringing them down to our level or worse; giving us time to catch up."

"But, they have the ability to hit us in much the same way, don't they?" Adrian asked it like a question, but it was a statement. "They have ICBMs and submarine-launched nuclear missiles. If we launch on them, they launch on us. So we use nukes as the last option. We would win in number of strikes launched... it would end the war. But they would counter-attack and we would sustain a great deal of damage. That would basically destroy us both, so I only want to consider that option if it comes to the point that we recognize that we can't win. But, I want to maintain that capability for immediate use if needed. We have a great deal more nukes than they do."

Adrian took a sip of his coffee. "They're also involved in wars with Russia, Korea, India, and Japan. Wars they're winning, but they have to keep most of their nukes in reserve because Russia and India have their own nukes. Russia has a huge stockpile of nuclear weapons and China doesn't."

"The next question to consider is whether or not making that plain to the Chinese leadership would avert the war. If I called up their Chairman and told him point blank that we will launch an all-out nuclear attack on his homeland if the invasion attempt isn't called off – would he call it off? And if he did, for how long? They couldn't have started this without fully considering that possibility. I have to believe that they are willing to bet – are already betting – that we won't launch. Calling them up and threatening them won't do any good, and it won't stop the invasion. So I don't see any reason to even try it. Better to keep silent and let them worry about it on their own. They already know that they face a mutual suicide situation, no need for me to tell them what they already know."

Adrian fell silent, in deep thought again. Linda came into the kitchen and sat down with them. She saw the strain on Adrian's face and asked, "What's the latest then? It can't be good from your expression."

Slowly Adrian looked up and into Linda's eyes. "It amounts to this; China is going to hit us with an overwhelmingly large number of ships and soldiers, numbers that we don't have a chance of stopping.

We can launch nukes on them now or later, but in either case they'll retaliate – and they have enough nuclear capability to do too much damage to us to risk it. So, either we figure out a way to beat them without nukes, or we surrender, or we commit suicide by nuking them out. So we have to figure out a way to beat them."

Adrian smiled at Linda and continued, "And I think I have an idea." At this announcement Adrian stood up. "Admiral, I need to go for a walk and talk this over with Linda. I want to see what she thinks of my half-baked notion. If she thinks it has a chance, I'll get back with you and we'll get the ball rolling."

The Admiral stood. "I'll come back for dinner and you can let me know then. And Adrian... I hope it's a damn good idea, because I am at my wits end for ideas right now."

As Linda and Adrian strolled through the village, Adrian explained his plan. "Their navy and ours are more or less evenly matched right now. We're better equipped, and have far better attack and defense systems. In a straight up fight we'd win. The Chinese know that, so it won't be a straight up fight. Their primary advantage is that they can resupply their weapons with ammunition. They are making replacement missiles and torpedoes and we aren't. One of the first things they fired back up after the solar storm was ammunition manufacturing. They are years ahead of us on that. Right now we can't even make a single new .22 caliber bullet. So if I was them, the tactic I would use would be to push as many targets at us as they can, sacrificial targets they can stand to lose, hoping we'll use up our finite armament supply and then... then their fleet has the advantage."

As they walked they came to Matt's blacksmith shop. They found Matt busy working on yet another new invention. Matt saw Adrian and Linda approach and greeted them with a large smile. "Hey guys! You out for a stroll or did you come to see me on purpose?"

Adrian shook Matt's large hand and clapped him on the shoulder. "A bit of both actually. I want to ask your opinion on something." Adrian explained what he had in mind, then he and Matt and Linda talked about it for half an hour, bouncing ideas back and forth. Matt made a quick sketch as Adrian watched, then said, "Something like this?"

"Yes." Adrian said, something like that indeed. "Can I borrow this? I want to show it to the Admiral tonight."

"It's all yours Adrian, let me know if there is any way at all I can help."

Adrian rolled the sketch up and replied "If you could make a detailed drawing along with instructions and specifications on the same sheet that would be a tremendous help... especially if you could figure out some way to make several hundred copies."

"The drawing is easy... several hundred copies..." he scratched his head. "That'll take some thinking. I'll cypher on it and get back to you as soon as I have an idea. You kids enjoy the evening as best you can. Oh, and Adrian, you need to know that I, we all, understand the tremendous load on your shoulders and that we all have faith that you're the best possible person to see us through this. We know it's hard... just wanted you to know." Matt finished with an embarrassed smile at his less- than-adept way of expressing himself.

As they walked slowly back home, they came across a number of their friends and stopped to chat briefly with each of them before detouring to the horse pasture. Horses were fairly rare these days, most of them having been eaten during the great famine that followed the grid dropping. Whenever he could, Adrian bartered for horses, adding them to the slowly growing remuda. Taking a bucket of corn from the feed shed, he and Linda stood at the fence and lovingly hand fed the horses that came up to greet them. It was an almost daily ritual, visiting the horses in the evening.

Adrian and Linda stood side by side, not talking, not needing to talk – taking a short break from the hardness they faced. *These are the best moments*, Adrian reflected. *The horses taking food from our hands, sunset glowing red in the west, quiet... just a few bird calls as the night birds take over from the day birds. The rumbling of the horses jaws as they eat the hard corn, their aroma, pungent, yet pleasing in an earthy way. The woman I love standing quietly beside me, knowing my thoughts, sharing this with me. These fleeting moments of deep and simple pleasure sustain. This is the way it should be all the time...*

CHAPTER 4

BACK AT THE KITCHEN TABLE, Adrian and the Admiral were once again seated along with Matt, Perry, Roman and Tim. Sarah and Linda had also joined them.

Adrian said, "I have an idea, but I have to put it into perspective for it to make sense, so bear with me a bit. When the solar storm wiped out the world's electricity grids, civilization as we knew it went down the tubes over-night. We had become too dependent on a vulnerable electric supply system. Everything depended on electricity, and to top that off our food supply and distribution system was too centralized... food had to be shipped from distant places on a daily basis. When that was interrupted mass starvation quickly followed.

"Third world countries fared better than we did – many of them were basically unaffected. Then there's China – halfway between a third world and first world country, their population almost evenly split between agriculture and industrial. When the gird dropped, the Chinese government forced everyone out of the cities, out onto the farms. It was hard, but it worked and most of their citizens survived... they didn't face the famine we did."

Adrian stood up and began slowly pacing the

room as he talked. "As soon as they were stabilized they began bringing select people back to the cities. Engineers and skilled workers, and thousands of trainees. They began rebuilding their electric infrastructure, and as each area was powered up they brought factories back on line. They concentrated on the areas that would do the most good for them... including the shipyards. The major constraint for them has been fuel for their power plants. They were a net fuel importer before the grid dropped, and quickly reached growth capacity based on their own internal resources. To continue their progress they need more fuel. Primarily they need refined oil."

Adrian sat down again. "They took over all the oil fields they could reach – the off-shore oil platforms were the easiest to take – but they weren't nearly enough. They also have a shortage of refineries to turn crude oil into fuels. The obvious solution for them is to look at us... thousands of sources of oil, thousands of miles of pipelines, hundreds of refineries... a greatly weakened Navy... and no centralized government running the show. Pretty much all they have to do is show up and take over, then they can send refined fuels back to the homeland as fast as they can load the tankers and turn them around.

"Their Navy is no match for our Navy, even under these circumstances. We have superior weaponry. On their side though, they can resupply their armaments and we can't. Once we've depleted our supply of munitions, we're helpless and they can shoot us out of the water at will. But first they have to get us to shoot until we run dry, and shoot at targets other than their Navy. They have amassed a huge armada of commercial ships, and have virtually unlimited manpower to put on those ships. I believe that what they are going to do is load up all of those commercial ships with as many soldiers as each ship can carry, launch them all at us, at both coast lines, and spread them out as far apart as they can in the process.

"They know that we can't afford to let those ships land and deploy their soldiers onto our shores. They believe we'll use up our munitions stopping that invasion. It's a war of attrition – they'll sacrifice as many ships and men as it takes to force us to deplete our fighting ability. Then their Navy moves in and destroys our Navy. Once our Navy is destroyed we've lost the war and they can land and take over any place they want to. Not only will this give them access to all the fuel they want, it also gives them a base to launch attacks on the rest of this hemisphere. It's a simple plan, one that can't fail for them. Their only true gamble in this is whether we will launch nuclear weapons against them. My guess is that once the ships are launched and on the way they'll contact us with some kind of bargain. But it won't be a bargain they intend to keep.

"So, our only chance of maintaining our independence and our resources, is to win this war without using either our naval munitions or nuclear weapons. We have to win it with an unconventional approach. Think along the lines of how guerilla warfare against a large conventional military works. That's the approach I've been thinking of."

The Admiral interrupted. "But... how? We're not

talking about a situation where hit-and-run tactics will make any difference. They are already willing to sacrifice as many of their ships and men as it takes. They'll just keep coming and overwhelm us with numbers."

"You're almost right Admiral... almost." Adrian replied. He stood and began pacing again. "These sacrifice ships are commercial ships. They are not heavily armored, hell they're not armored at all. They are fragile. They might mount some defensive weapons on them, but it won't be much... and if my plan works it won't matter what they can shoot. We're going to come at them in a way they don't expect, and will be hard-pressed to defend against... which will leave our Navy fully prepared and waiting for their Navy... assuming they don't recall their Navy before we can get at them."

Adrian stepped up to the table and unrolled the drawing that Matt had made earlier that day, placing cups at the corners to keep it from rolling back up. "Take a look at this Admiral."

The Admiral removed a pair of reading glasses from his shirt pocket, put them on, and began studying the simple drawing. After a moment he said, "I see what you've drawn, but I don't follow what you're thinking."

"Guerilla warfare on the open seas Admiral. What you're looking at is a representation of a typical outboard-powered small pleasure boat. About eighteen feet of boat driven by a one-hundred horsepower outboard engine. At the front of the boat is an improvised explosive device, made from one of the hundreds-of-thousands of field artillery rounds in warehouses around the country. Could be about any size round, but I'm thinking about a 120mm round set to explode on contact. Fill the rest of the boat with explosives, and send it like a missile against a commercial ship. We'd control it by a radio remote control, like radio-controlled airplanes.

"There must be a million of these small craft up and down our shores. The radio control systems are easy to make and to operate. We also have thousands of commercial and fishing ships available. Get those ships operational, including their radars, load each ship with as many of these radio controlled artillery shell boats as it can hold, and sail forth. Using the radar, locate and close in on the Chinese craft... get within visual range and launch one or two of these boats. Then steer the boats into the Chinese ship by remote control and make a big hole in it. Aiming at the rudder would be the best... even if the ship doesn't sink, it will be foundered where it floats."

Adrian was again pacing the room while everyone stared at him, listening intently. "If we can get enough of these in action soon enough, we can do serious damage, maybe even stop the invasion at sea without using up our munitions in the process. The challenge isn't whether or not this will work; the challenge is getting enough boats on the water loaded with these radio controlled boats in time to get the job done." Adrian sat back down, waiting for the reaction.

"Damn." The Admiral said quietly. Then he began to smile. Then he laughed. "Damn. Adrian its genius! It's pure, bloody genius. You're right, those ships are not built to withstand a direct explosion.

Just one or two hits can sink most of them, and hitting them in the rudder even makes sinking them unnecessary, although I think that would sink most of them anyway. Damn! We can sink them all without losing one of our own in the process." Then, more soberly the Admiral said "You're also right about the challenge though. Getting enough of these made, all up and down the coast, is going to be the real challenge here. How do you think we're going to do that?"

Adrian replied, "We set up six locations on each coast where boats can be quickly retrofitted. We send out by runner a set of code keys that are to be distributed by hand across the country as fast as possible. I'll come back to that in a minute. When we have the code keys distributed – and that has to happen very fast – we'll broadcast by ham radio across the country, in code, the entire story of what we're up against. The full story, the full set of choices. We ask for help from all former Americans to get to the shore, gather up as many boats as they can, and take them to their closest retrofit location. Others are to break into warehouses to get the materials to multiple locations that we'll identify. We'll send trucks or helicopters to gather the materials at those collection points, and take them to the nearest retrofit location."

Adrian paused for a long moment. "The key is to mobilize every able-bodied person in this country. We have to depend on their judgment that our assessment and response are correct. If they believe us, if we don't keep any secrets about this operation, we just might pull it off. First we have to reach them in code. We have to move so fast that if the Chinese break the code it won't matter," Adrian stood without realizing it. "We have to put these boats together and get them out there and hit the invasion fleet before the Chinese can figure out what happened. If they figure it out too soon, they'll figure out a defense, and the whole game will change – and not in our favor."

Linda saw the raw intensity of Adrian at that moment. *His body is as rigid as iron, muscles popping like he's in a hard workout. He's on a mission now, a full-out, no holds barred, kill-the-enemy-right-now, mission. He has his plan in mind and is launching it, right here, right now. My God, that intensity is chilling, I wouldn't want to be a Chinese out there on that ocean... they're already dead. And he is going to pull this nation together in a way that none of us could ever have imagined.*

Adrian looked at Linda, he could see what she was thinking as clear as day. He gave her a little smile, then turned back to the table.

"Here's the detailed plan." Adrian unrolled a large scale highway map of the former United States.

CHAPTER 5

RACE SADDLED HER HORSE AND slung her gear over the back of the saddle. She picked up the rifle leaning on the corral rail and shoved it tightly into the leather scabbard that had been specifically designed for it. She double checked the saddle bag full of code sheets, each printed on waterproof paper. The bag also contained a map showing the known locations of ham operators in her assigned area. Having already said her goodbyes, she effortlessly lifted herself into the saddle, and hit the horse's flanks with her heels. It took off at a fast trot, Bear loping along behind.

This horse's peculiar trot was jarring for the rider, but natural to the horse, and was a pace she knew the horse could keep up all day. Race knew what to do: she fully relaxed all the muscles in her body not actually needed for keeping her in the saddle, and semi-relaxed all of the muscles she did need. It took practice to do that, a certain kind of posture in the saddle, the posture seen in old paintings of cowboys at work. A slumping kind of look. A casual, yet athletic pose. When the rider is seen in motion, the watcher would see that the rider never seemed to be moving yet the horse was all over the place. The rider relaxed into the stride, anticipating each move before it arrived, adjusted for it and rode it out smooth, using the least amount of energy possible. Muscles that flowed with the motion did not tire at anything like the pace of muscles that are stiff and resisting. Race rode easy in the saddle, which would have been high praise from the old cowboys.

"First a Ranger, and now Pony Express rider." She ruminated on the past three day's events as she rode. The night of Adrian's meeting with the Admiral she was roused from her bed and told to assemble the Rangers that were at hand, and summon all other Rangers back to base, from wherever they were, whatever they were doing.

"Tell them to drop whatever they are doing and return immediately as fast as possible." The messenger nearly glowed with an electric excitement. "We're going to war, and it starts right now. We're already behind, and we have to move. You'll get a full briefing as soon as you're assembled."

Adrian briefed them himself, in full. "...alright, now you know the big picture. You're going to play what is possibly the most vital part of the whole operation: getting those code keys spread as fast as you possibly can."

The growl of the Admiral's helicopter interrupted Adrian for a moment as it lifted off and quickly turned south-east towards Corpus Christi, taking him back to his aircraft carrier.

Adrian resumed, "You'll be given individual maps that show where to find ham operators in your area. You'll be provided sets of documents to disburse. The first document is a written briefing just as I gave you; it will be in plain English. It will not describe our preemptive battle plan. The second sheet is the code key and the instructions for using it. The Admiral has gone to get those created for you and will be back in less than two days. Believe me he's burning up his radio right now issuing instructions."

Adrian paused and looked at each Ranger directly, giving each a full three seconds of pure attention. He was looking them over, but mostly checking their eyes, he wanted to make sure each and every one was getting the message. He saw young eyes, intense eyes, intelligent eyes. Young faces filled with a sudden intensity of purpose. He knew he was seeing the future, and it humbled him, he felt ancient in front of these young men and women, even though he had only twenty years on them. "You'll ask each ham operator to check your map and fill in any missed locations. Also advise them to maintain radio silence on this and wait for the initiating broadcast from the war's headquarters, the Admiral's ship, at exactly midnight four days from now. This will all be explained in the briefing document, but remind them again to not discuss it over the air. Face-to-face though... they need to recruit runners and spread the message as far and wide as possible, but only by word of mouth. They have to tell everyone they can what's happening. ."

Adrian paused again to gather his thoughts. The Rangers didn't move, didn't speak. They were rigid with fascination.

"You won't have reached many operators before our initial broadcast, so you'll have to keep going as fast as you can and distribute the documents to every station on your map. When you're finished return as fast as you can for your next assignment. Speed is everything. Speed is the only defense we have right now. Every second you save counts, and counts a hell of a lot. You won't be able to stay more than half an hour at any station, you have to keep moving. I cannot stress enough that speed is our only chance. Speed is the imperative."

He paused to let the message sink in. For a moment the only sounds were those of crickets and the frogs in the nearby creek.

"Start seeing to your gear. As soon as you get your map study it until you have your locations memorized. If you lose the map you have to be able to keep going. Memorize your map and know it like you know your own home. We're going to use every vehicle we have in this, and all of the horses. You'll each be on your own when you leave. Double check your vehicles for maintenance issues and correct them. Load up with the tools and spare parts you're most likely to need. Tend to your horses, feed them up the next three days, exercise them gently, they're about to get a world-class workout. When the documents arrive I want all of you out of here in ten minutes. Dismissed!"

"Yep." Race thought to herself. *"Hell of a way to wake up."*

Strapped around Race's thin waist and tied to her right thigh was an old style six-shooter. As she rode, Race recalled how she had come across it at a barter shop and had become entranced with its simple but elegant design, and its possibilities. She paid dearly for the gun, holster and belt, two boxes of shells, a die for casting bullets, and a portable reloading kit that had been made in the pre-grid days. As long as she could find primers, powder, and lead she could keep a good supply of bullets on hand.

The pistol was a reproduction of Colt's 1878, double stage, .45 caliber, popularly known as the Peacemaker. Rugged, reliable, simple to maintain, and exceedingly deadly against humans at close range. It had the virtue of firing each time the trigger was drawn back. Every time. It was up to the operator to count the shots though, and Race always counted her shots. When she looked at the pistol in the barter shop she recognized its value as a close quarter's weapon. She Race often confronted men twice her size and twice her strength. She worked hard to keep confrontations at a distance that nullified their advantages of size and strength, but it didn't always happen that way. Her go-to close in weapon had been a knife, and when she was at arm's length, the knife was still her first choice. But at an intermediate range, a knife was useless. In certain situations there was no better weapon than a pistol that could be rapidly put into action, and the reproduction Colt 1878, double stage, .45 caliber, Peacemaker was rugged, reliable, simple to maintain, and exceedingly deadly at close range.

Race was about to have another need to use it.

After she had obtained the pistol she fired it six times as fast as she could, and then took it immediately to Matt. "I need to have this worked on Matt. It's stiff and has a hard trigger pull. I want to be able to draw it fast and shoot slick as owl snot."

Silently, but with a small smile, Matt took the pistol in his large hand. Removing the shells he dry fired it three times. "Yeah, it is a bit sticky. You run and fetch Tim, I'll need his advice, he knows all about these old guns. He used to be in quick draw contests with these things, way back in the day. He'll be able to teach you how to fast draw, set your holster up right, that sort of thing." It never occurred to Matt to question why a young woman would feel the need to be able to draw fast – the world had changed, and the survivor's mindset had followed, at times even predicted, that world.

Tim said, "Very nice work. Excellent condition. Impeccable design. You probably couldn't have chosen a better and more time proven weapon. It has speed, six opportunities, accurate within its intended range, and tons of stopping power. Set this up correctly and learn how to use it correctly and I'd put you against any other pistol and rig out there." Tim explained to Matt and Race how to adjust the pistol, how to get the smoothest operation on the trigger, and about buffing all moving parts to a better than mirror finish. "It's not a finicky weapon, but the friction between moving parts must be at an absolute minimum for speed shooting."

"Also file off that front sight, it's never used in speed shooting and can get caught on things. Shave the top first inch of the barrel just a hair, tapering the end of the top of the barrel, gives just a whisker of a faster draw as the barrel clears the holster. You'll have to rework these grips...these are too large for Race's hand. Sand them down to fit her hand perfectly. There are a lot of hours of work involved here, but the results will be worth every bit of it. When you're finished, give me the gun and the rig. I'll modify the belt and holster. I'll bone in the holster to the pistol, cut down the front of the holster as much as possible and position the holster properly on the belt. Race, when we're done you won't believe the difference... it's as though we're changing a Volkswagen into a Ferrari. Once everything is together I'll teach you the basics, then the advanced techniques. You're going to be a walking death machine."

"That's the idea." Race replied. "That's exactly the idea, and I appreciate the hell out of both of you for this."

"Aw, you're like a daughter to us – well a granddaughter to that old codger." Matt replied while hooking a thumb towards Tim.

"Exactly like a granddaughter." Tim replied with a genuine smile.

Race wasn't prepared for the rush of emotion those words caused to whirl around in her head. Rarely caught speechless, she quickly hugged each of the men and then almost ran off in her sudden embarrassment. She was overwhelmed.

A sudden change in the horses gait brought Race's attention fully focused in the present. She didn't see anything to alarm the horse, yet it had altered its gait to a more cautious one. She didn't doubt the horse's senses for a second. She gently tapped the flanks with her heels and the horse regained its normal jarring gait. Race scanned the surrounding trees and shrubs without seeming to be too interested. Bear was out of sight somewhere, but he often disappeared into the brush. Casually she slipped the holding loop from the hammer of her pistol and held the reins in her left hand, resting her right hand on her thigh just above the pistol's grip.

CHAPTER 6

THREE MEN JUMPED OUT OF the brush in front of her. She wheeled the horse to a sideways stop with the horse's right side to the men so that she had a clear field of fire. Race could hardly believe her eyes – this close to Fort Brazos and these yahoos thought they were going to take her horse, and no doubt a hell of a lot more. One had a shotgun, the other two rifles.

They're confident they can handle a girl. They held their weapons casually, only one was pointed in her direction. *He'll be first,* she thought. *Then the shotgun on the right, and last the rifle on the left. Center, right, left.* She pictured this in her mind's eye as one of the men told her to get off the horse. She was as cool as a pool hustler lining up shots.

Race had practiced and shot enough to know that she could kill all three men before they got off a shot. She had time on her side, yet she was in a hurry to get going again. As the man finished speaking she slid the pistol from the holster. She didn't raise the pistol at arm's length, nor even halfway. She fired just as Tim had taught her, gun just at the top of the holster, arm slightly back and elbow bent. The tiny adjustments needed to put the bullet into the target were automatic, drilled in to her by

Tim's training and lots of practice. They required absolutely no thought at all. She fired center, the hammer seeming to fall in slow motion. As soon as the hammer struck she was moving on to the next target while pulling back smoothly on the trigger. She reached the intuitive point of aim at exactly the moment the hammer dropped again. She saw Bear as a brown blur rocketing out of the brush at the man on the left.

Now her biggest traverse, from all the way right to all the way left. It seemed to take forever, but she didn't rush it, she knew she had all the time in the world. Smoothly she moved the barrel into line with the third target, and as before the hammer dropped exactly when she knew she was on target. Only the third man, the one on the left, had had time to begin to bring his rifle up, but Bear had launched into the air and ripped at the man's arm. Race could have beaten him from a standstill, but Bear made it easy for her. She sat there a second, listening to the echo of the gunshots roll off into the trees. She reloaded the three spent shells, carefully keeping the brass.

The horse had been trained for this, and had stood dead still at the first gunshot. Race clucked her tongue and ticked it with her heels and they took off again at that gut-wrenching gait. Race didn't look back, she didn't need to. Every minute was precious, and she had lost time that she had to make up now. It never occurred to her that she hadn't spoken a single word to the three men.

She rode late into the night before stopping to rest the horse. She unsaddled and rubbed it down, feeding it a hat full of corn that she had brought along, then walked it to the spring and watered it. When it was finished, she hobbled it so that it could graze and drink freely while she slept. Unrolling her bedroll she lay down with the saddle under her head and chewed a piece of jerky with occasional sips of water. She fed Bear two pieces of the jerky – although he was adept at keeping himself well fed, she enjoyed sharing her meals with him.

She slept until just before grey streaks of sunrise began to show. One thing about having Bear in the camp, she could sleep soundly knowing he would give her plenty of notice if someone approached. On waking she stood and then did a dozen deep knee bends to unkink her muscles, saddled the horse and was on the trail again within minutes. Breakfast was another piece of jerky eaten in the saddle. Chewing jerky while riding in the jolting horse's gait took talent to keep from biting her tongue.

Within three hours she arrived at her first ham station. A querulous old man with long gray hair and a huge matted beard appeared at the door. She gave him a quick rundown on the situation then handed over the documents he would need. They talked for a few moments then Race was ready to move on to the next station. "What you mean you can't stay to explain? I'm just supposed to take your word for all this?"

"Chuck," Race replied patiently, "I've gone over it twice and I know you understand. You just want company. And while I'd love to sit and talk, I have to get going. Spread the word as fast as you can. Don't radio ahead to let Stan know I'm on my way, too many ears and too many chances to set up an ambush if they know where I'll be. There's a ton of people out there that want me dead, don't help them any please." With a quick smile that melted the old man's resistance she whirled the horse and was off at a gallop. As soon as she was out of sight she returned the horse to his infernal gait.

Adrian felt the jet's wheels hit the runway and breathed a sigh of relief. He was far too big to be comfortable in the back seat of the F-16D, and hadn't been able to so much as scratch for the last two hours. The ride had been tolerable other than that. The pilot had flown a smooth and stable flight from Corpus Christi to the submarine base at New London, Connecticut. Adrian was making a tour of the east coast staging points. This location was the first stop because it had already begun retro-fitting pleasure boats into guided surface torpedoes, and Adrian wanted to be on-hand to see the first test run.

As he inched his way out of the cockpit and climbed down to the runway surface a Navy Captain stood at attention waiting for him. "Welcome to Connecticut, Mr. President!" The Captain shouted over the subsiding sound of the jet's engines. He snapped off a smart salute to Adrian.

Adrian smiled and returned the salute. "Thank you. Captain...?"

"Bryant sir. The Jeep will take us to the terminal where you can refresh, and then we'll go straight to the test location, sir."

"That's thoughtful and much appreciated Captain Bryant. Let's get rolling."

Adrian and the Captain settled in the Jeep and the driver roared off, the pilot staying with his aircraft. A scant half-hour later, they were standing on a pier at the naval base looking down at what had once been a rather typical twenty-foot ski boat. Everything from the outboard motor forward had been stripped, and the hull packed with explosives. Mounted on the prow was a 105mm artillery shell with a contact detonator. Mounted on the shell was a video camera. The outboard was equipped with a set of levers, linkages and servo motors along with a radio receiver.

"As you can see Mr. President, the boat is a bomb with enormous explosive potential. We've added a video camera so the operator can see the target from the boat's perspective. He steers the boat with a radio control device that has a range of about twenty miles, depending on conditions. It's a simple but robust system made from components available in an almost endless supply. There must be millions of boats like these, the radio control devices are easy to find or make, and the steering linkage is so simple any teenager could make them from scratch. We've stacked the explosives as best we can into a more or less shape charge so that more of the explosive power surges forward towards the target, instead of just blowing up in a general fashion. The shape charge effect is crude given what we have to work with, but better than not doing it."

"Why the det cord?" Adrian asked.

"We're pretty sure we don't need it, but to be on the safe side we've wrapped det cord around the artillery shell and then led it back to various points in the explosives. It's just a precaution, but it only takes a few minutes to install and will assure complete detonation of all of the explosives. Ready to see it run?" Captain Bryant replied.

"Absolutely."

"Tow it out!" Bryant shouted to the crew in the tow boat. The tow boat slowly pulled the explosives boat out into the bay, then untied the line from it and returned to the dock.

Turning to Adrian, Bryant said "The target is that old freighter across the bay. If we sink it, no harm done. We're going to run the explosives boat from the tow boat, so you'll be able to watch the operator, the explosive boat, and the target."

As Adrian watched, a sailor on the tow boat opened an aluminum case. A video monitor was mounted in the top half and the bottom half contained a series of on/off switches, buttons, a rheostat like knob, and a simple, toggle-style directional controller. The sailor began flipping switches, first powering up the device, then turning on the explosives boat's engine and beginning to maneuver it across the bay. Using his right hand on the toggle he moved the boat around in a series of maneuvers. Once he had completed the maneuvers to his satisfaction he turned the boat towards the target in a long arc, while simultaneously increasing the outboard's speed to maximum.

The boat roared across the bay rising to a smooth plane, leaving a rooster tail and a white wake clearly visible against the blue water. Adrian watched with intense interest, his gaze switching back and forth from the boat itself to the image on the viewscreen, as the boat made short work of crossing the bay and slammed into the middle of the target freighter. There was a huge explosion as it made contact and water shot upwards, temporarily obscuring their view of the impact area. Slowly the water fell back down and they were able to see a twenty-foot hole in the freighter's hull, and water rapidly pouring into the old freighter. Within minutes the freighter had settled into the mud below, less than half its topside showing above the small waves of the bay.

"Outstanding work gentlemen!" Adrian said with obvious pleasure. "Let's go see the assembly process."

Later that evening, Adrian was in Myrtle Beach South Carolina for the same kind of review. Adrian had decided to meet with the local militia leaders while making these inspections, and had a local ham operator call ahead and make the arrangements. He wanted them at the pier to see the demonstrations for themselves. The demonstrations, and the meetings, were both successful, and he continued a three week tour of each of the twelve rallying locations, meeting with everyone that cared to come. Each successive meeting drew larger crowds than the one before as word spread that he was making the tour. At his final stop, in Los Angeles, the crowd measured in the thousands. Adrian gave them the same speech he had given at the other locations.

Adrian was a natural orator. He had a deep booming voice that easily carried to the farthest reaches of the crowd. He spoke slowly, clearly enunciating each word so that listeners could easily keep up with the speech. He had a gift for knowing when to raise his volume and when to lower it. His unconscious talent for keeping an audience engaged was dramatically efficient.

"I'll keep this short because no one likes a long speech. In a very short time, we will be under attack by the Chinese. Time is our first enemy, and the Chinese are the second. We have solid information that the Chinese need our oil and refineries and that they intend to take them by force. But they won't stop there. Our once-great country still has an untold wealth of resources that they need. Iron, copper, oil, coal, natural gas, farmland, space, infrastructure that they can repair and operate... to them, we're a strategic base for taking over the entire hemisphere. They'll take the off-shore drilling platforms and coastal refineries first. But make no mistake, they won't stop there. They'll continue inland until they have taken everything. They'll bring in millions and millions of soldiers, engineers and workers to permanently inhabit our land. From there, eventually, they'll move north and south into the rest of the countries in this hemisphere. For the Chinese, this is a great opportunity, one they never dreamed of having. If they wait too long, they may not be able to get a foothold, so they're moving now.

"Our best chance is to defeat them on the oceans. They are far more vulnerable out there than they will be if they establish beachheads. So we intend to stop them out there, and we need the help of every man and woman on this continent to do it. We have to be organized. Working hard isn't enough by itself, we also have to work exceedingly *fast*. Please get yourselves organized into four basic groups. Group one is to find and bring boats, explosives, radio-controllers, closed circuit TV systems, and skilled workers to the assembly point. Group two will be the skilled workers that take those materials and produce the explosive boats. Group three will be a land-based militia ready to travel to wherever the Chinese might slip by the naval operation and fight them on land. Group four will be the commercial ships and the crews that take the fight to the enemy on the high seas.

"After we've won this war, we need to organize a nation again. I say this because *we will win this war*! And you will have become organized enough to create your own Republic. We have established a working Republic in Texas, complete with a new constitution. Any State that adopts a constitution like ours – establishing their own Republic with the same laws as ours – will be invited to join a mutual defense pact. This defense pact will be crafted by a joint resolution of all of the Republics into an alliance. Unlike the former federal government that ultimately failed us, we will utilize a set of agreements on mutual defense and trade. Each Republic will be independent, on its own; self-sufficient, and beholden only to its own citizens."

CHAPTER 7

ADRIAN CONTINUED FROM THE TWO coast lines to the interior. Word was spread where he would be and for anyone that could to meet up with him. Mostly he chose major cross-roads of the interstate highway system, for their easy public access and the stretch of clear highway where the jet fighter could land and refuel from bladders supplied by the Navy. By the time Adrian completed his rounds he was exhausted and never wanted to see the inside of an F-16 again as long as he lived.

He wanted to sleep for seven days, but slept only seven hours before he was back at work again, meeting with the Admiral who had flown up from Corpus Christi. Sitting at the kitchen table with Adrian, the Admiral said "We're broadcasting coded messages continuously, now. The reports we're getting back reflect that the word is out, and people know what to do. There is a massive surge of people heading for the twelve coastal points, raiding warehouses and armories as they go. Boats are being taken from thousands of locations and being moved. We'll have close to three thousand of them ready within a couple of weeks. Merchant craft to take the explosive boats out to sea and deploy them are being worked on by the dozens, I estimate we'll have four or five hundred of them ready to go soon. Scores are already operational and loaded with explosive boats, waiting for the signal to go.

"Believe it or not, our biggest obstacle is lack of navigational skills. Astral navigation is almost a lost art. The Navy kept the training at a high standard, but nearly everyone else relied on GPS navigation – and of course the GPS satellites were fried by the CME. We have naval personnel at each of the twelve locations running navigation classes continuously, and we'll have a cadre of trained navigators ready to go when the ships are ready. Radio codes for ship-to-ship and ship-to-shore communications are in place... but I still have questions about your strategy and tactics I'd like you to clear up."

"Go ahead Admiral, ask all the questions you want." Adrian said.

"Well first, why do you think the Chinese will hit our east coast? The west coast is a straight line shot for them. Other than our ships in Hawaii they won't have any obstacles. The east coast will require them to go around the tip of Africa, or through the Arctic passage. They can't get through the Panama Canal – there's no power for the locks – and the Suez Canal would be too dangerous, their ships would be too easy to attack from land. They have a hell of a long way to go to get to the east coast, so why bother?"

Adrian replied, "The Chinese are experts at warfare, they've had thousands of years of practice at it. I've been putting myself in their place, tried thinking it through their way. If I were them, and didn't know about our counter-attack plans, I'd try to draw all of the former US Navy into as small

EDEN'S WAR

an area as possible, with the obvious place being centered on Hawaii. That would leave the back door weakly guarded, and that's where I would send my main force.

"Distraction is a wonderful thing if you can pull it off, then you can make a surprise attack where they're not looking. The Chinese will have their fleets moving through the Arctic Circle and around the tip of Africa long before they show themselves in the Pacific – they may already be en route. In the meantime they'll engage us near Hawaii, try to draw off as much of the Navy into a battle as they can, then they'll spread out far and wide across the Pacific Ocean to lure our Navy after them. About that time – while we're engaged in the Pacific Theater, their other two fleets will be hitting up and down the Atlantic Coast. If you had any high flying spy planes, I believe you'd spot those two fleets – if I don't miss my guess, they're about three weeks or less from coming around the corners."

The Admiral nodded thoughtfully, and Adrian continued.

"What they won't expect is for our Navy to hang back, saving our munitions while our Civilian Navy – which they don't know about – goes out and sinks the majority of their decoy tankers and freighters. We will use attrition in a way they don't expect, eliminating their advance fleet and leaving their Navy exposed to our fully loaded naval ships. *Then* it will be your turn Admiral. Our Navy will go after theirs, probably chasing them all the way back to China to sink them all. That'll give us many years to bring our own country back up to a point we

55

can more readily defend it. To a point where their window of opportunity has closed." Adrian stood up and began pacing the room.

"Another reason is that the west coast has more off-shore oil wells and coastal refineries, it's a target rich environment, which makes it almost too obvious. The Gulf of Mexico alone is a treasure house of oil sources and refineries, although I don't expect them to strike there first."

"Why not?" The Admiral asked.

Adrian paused his pacing. "They won't want to be trapped in the gulf with an opposing Navy that is healthy, it's too small of an area. I think they'll go for a feint within a feint instead. They'll time it so that their North Atlantic fleet strikes first across the Atlantic seaboard. They'll have open ocean to maneuver in and thousands of miles of coastline to work with. They'll hope to draw out and diminish our Navy in the Pacific before they move into the confines of the gulf. Their southern fleet will slip into the Gulf after the northern fleet has occupied most of our Atlantic Navy."

"How confident are you of these predictions Adrian?"

Adrian stopped pacing. "How confident can anyone be, Admiral? All I know for sure is that if I were them, that's what I would do. I can sum up for you the entire history of man in a simple analogy, and it applies here as well. Imagine a locked room with two starving men in it. A hatch opens and a steak is thrown in between the two men. Only if the two men are of even strength and fighting ability will they share the steak. But if one man is stronger than the other, the strong man will eat the entire steak. After he's eaten the steak, and the two men are sitting on opposite sides of the room staring at each other, the stronger man realizes that sooner or later he's going to have to sleep – and when he does the weaker man will attack while he has the advantage. So the stronger man kills the weaker man in a pre-emptive strike".

Adrian pulled his chair out and turned it around, sitting on it backwards with his arms draped over the chair's back. "We are the weaker man in that room. We have little organization, few people and poor communications, but... it's a wide room and we are sitting on the steak. China has the exquisite organization that only a brutal dictatorship can muster, more people than it needs, and it wants the steak. The ocean and distance between us more or less evens our strength. If they don't hit us now while we are at our weakest, we will eventually grow to the point they can't get the steak."

The Admiral, frowning, said, "And if you're wrong? If you're wrong we could be playing our cards against a completely unknown strategy. We could lose."

"I know, and it keeps me wide awake nights thinking about it. But no matter how I think it through, no matter what other strategies I come up with... I always come back to this one. If I'm wrong or if our plan doesn't work, then I've lost the war for all of us. I will have failed every man, woman, and child in this country, led them down a bitter path of ruination. I can barely breathe sometimes from the pressure of making these decisions. My only solace is in General Patton's belief that a good plan violently executed now is better than a perfect plan next week. I believe in that with every fiber of my being."

The Admiral responded, "I know the pressure on you is inhuman. I've never seen anyone's hair turn white as fast as yours these past weeks. I feel bad for having maneuvered you into this responsibility, but unfortunately for you there was no one better... no one even close. If it's any consolation, I would never in a million years have taken the approach to this war that you have. I would have approached it in a conventional manner, and probably have lost... assuming you're right of course, which I hope to God you are."

Adrian shifted his weight, making the chair creak. "Admiral, the only consolation possible is winning this war. If we don't win, my only other consolation, such as it would be, will be to die fighting. There's no way I could live with losing on my conscience. There's no way I could look anyone in the face ever again, and there's no way I would live under Chinese rule. I explained this to Linda... know what she said? She said *then you better win.*" Adrian smiled ruefully at the memory. "If you think I don't have more than enough pressure, try living up to that. So get out the maps and reports, let's go over them again."

Later that evening Adrian met with his kitchen cabinet, Matt, Tim, Perry, Linda, Roman and Sarah. "I've been worried that our civilian navy might, in the confusion of battle, mistakenly attack each other. They'll be out there with only radio communications seeking to destroy anything that looks like a commercial ship – and they'll be in commercial ships themselves. Mistaken identity would be disastrous. We need a simple way to identify the enemy, something the Chinese can't imitate when they figure out what kind of attack they're under. I'm drawing a blank, though. Any ideas?"

There was a long silence. Then Matt asked, "How about a coded sonar signal? Their Naval ships will have sonar receivers but it's not likely their commercial ships will. Our ships can be provided with one-time codes that change every day. One ship sends a signal query and the other ships send a coded reply. Sonar will give the direction and distance to the replies. Any ship not responding or not responding correctly will be a target."

Perry said, "That would work, but it does have some downsides. First, can we find and install enough sonar systems in time? Second... any Chinese ship hearing a sonar ping regardless of the code, will know to go to full defensive systems. Third, any Chinese naval ship equipped with sonar will be able to zero-in on the transmission locations, making our ships locations instantly known and thus vulnerable."

Matt replied, "True. You know we can automatically assume any tanker is enemy, we aren't putting tankers out there, so that leaves the other types of ships to consider. Flags are out because they are too easy to fake. Radio and flash signals are out for basically the same reasons as sonar." He paused, then looked up. "Our ships are all being equipped with medium range radar to spot enemy ships too far off to see. That also has its disadvantages, but they're necessary, and they are going to be used, and used a lot... so why not use them for friend-or-foe identification?"

Adrian asked, "How do we do that?"

Matt replied, "I'm sure the Admiral will know how to set it up, and if it can be set up in time. Can you reach him on the radio and ask?"

Minutes later Adrian was talking to the Admiral by encoded radio transmission. The Admiral was explaining "Yes, it's simple enough – we've been doing it since WWII. The fact that we'll have to be using radar anyway means we're not increasing the risk to our ships significantly. The real question is can we modify the existing radars on our ships in time. I'll talk it over with the experts... and if it can be done we'll contact the radar techs that are setting up the radars at the twelve shipyards and get them on it. I'll call you back in a couple of hours."

CHAPTER 8

ALTHOUGH ADRIAN WAS THE PRESIDENT of the Republic of Texas, had ultimate control of the former United States Armed Forces, and was leading the war against China, he still had to produce his own food for himself and Linda. By design, the new Republic's politicians garnered no salary of any kind. Adrian's family and friends had taken up most of the slack, tending the fields and the stock during his absence, but the smokehouse meat was running low, so Adrian went hog hunting. Feral hogs had been a problem in Texas before the grid went down. That problem was now a blessing, a ready supply of delicious meat, although a dangerous animal to hunt.

Going hunting also gave Adrian a brief respite from the grinding responsibilities he had unwillingly but dutifully taken on. A respite of but a few hours, but a few hours went a long way for him these days. He shed his politician life like a snake sheds skin. It was a huge relief to be on his own, in the woods again. He would have preferred to harvest smaller pigs because they were more tender and had better flavor, but with his time limitations he decided to kill one large hog instead. Borrowing one of Matt's efficient hog rifles, he donned his moccasin boots and walked into the forest. Adrian knew of a grove of oak trees the hogs regularly came to for acorns, a favored food. It had a source of water nearby and was far from any settler or settlement. It was a hog magnet.

The hogs had weak eyesight but made up for it with a keen sense of smell, so Adrian approached the oak grove from down-wind. He chose a tree between the southern edge of the grove and the water where they would eventually come to drink. Climbing the tree, he settled in for what he was sure would be a long wait, pleasantly surprised when a huge sow leading a dozen other feral hogs came trundling out of the oak grove almost immediately. They stopped here and there rooting around but were definitely heading for the water, and would soon provide an excellent opportunity for Adrian. Slowly shifting his position in the tree so that he would be able to shoot where he expected them to pass by, he smiled slightly. *Almost too easy,* he thought to himself.

Within a few minutes the hogs were moving towards the water at a fast walk. Adrian lined his sights just behind the shoulder of the lead sow, waiting for it to be in just the right position, to be a quartering away shot so that the large caliber bullet would penetrate from behind the thick gristle carapace. The bullet from this gun would penetrate that shield readily enough, it had been designed just for that purpose, but Adrian had an instinctive drive to be as efficient as possible. As the hog passed by, Adrian squeezed the trigger. The large caliber rifle boomed out, shattering the peaceful quiet. The hog ran three feet and dropped.

But just as the hog dropped the limb that Adrian was sitting on cracked and shattered, dropping Adrian twenty feet to the ground. He landed flat on his back, the wind driven from his lungs. He lay for a moment, fighting to remain conscious. The last thing he needed was to be unconscious with a pack of wild hogs nearby; they would eat him as fast as they would the acorns. Slowly he sat up, looking around for the rifle, grateful to find it near at hand. He picked it up just as he heard a crashing sound coming towards him from where he had last seen the hogs. They were stampeding as a result of the loud shot and crash of the falling branch, but in their confusion they were stampeding directly towards him. Looking up he saw a big boar with long, sharp tusks coming straight at him. Adrian was well aware of the danger he was now in, being on the ground with a wild boar was a bad bet all around. He rose to his knees, snapping the rifle up to his shoulder, and fired at the boar with a born rifleman's instinctive shooting style. The huge slug tore through the boar's head, blowing its brains outwards and backwards as the slug ripped on through boar's spinal column shattering it as it traveled half way down its back. The boar died running and slid to a stop just feet from Adrian.

Still unable to breathe fully from the fall, and a bit woozy, he used the rifle as a crutch and stood up. Immediately he reloaded the two chambers. Climbing back up the tree was out of the question for the moment. His best bet was to stand against the tree trunk and be still. Hopefully the other hogs would leave. That hope was shattered within seconds as another large boar came charging out of the short brush to his right. Again Adrian snapped up the rifle and fired, but the bullet's impact was at a shallow angle to the tough skull and slid along bone and exited. The boar barely flinched as it continued its charge. The rifle was already in position and still had one shot in it. Adrian took his time aiming, letting the hog get closer before firing again. The hog dropped, his head shattered. Adrian quickly reloaded. He waited and listened, his breath at last coming back in long ragged gasps, his head was clearing, though his ears rang with the echoes of the gunshots.

When it was clear that the rest of the hogs had gone, Adrian gutted the three hogs. Then he quartered the largest one and carried three of the quarters back to Fort Brazos. His back was sore from the fall but even under better circumstances it would have been a challenge to carry all of the first hog back in one trip. When he arrived home he dumped the meat on the butchering table and went to find help bringing the rest of the meat back. Later that night after he had completed the butchering and had the meat hanging in the smoke house curing under pecan wood smoke, he took a long hot shower, dressed in clean clothes, and sat down at the kitchen table with Linda and the Admiral who had choppered in to discuss the war preparations.

Adrian recounted his little adventure. Linda was concerned but refused to show it; she knew that Adrian was only trying to explain why he had brought back so much meat when he hadn't intended or needed to. So she smiled and acted amused, even though she was horrified at how a small accident came near to ending Adrian's life.

The Admiral, on the other hand, was aghast at Adrian's close call, and made no effort to hide it.

"Jesus Christ Adrian! What the hell were you thinking? We've got a major world war on our hands and you are the Commander in Chief! You're absolutely indispensable to the war, and on top of that are completely irreplaceable. There isn't another man in this country who can take your place – not one! And you go gallivanting around the country falling out of trees and tackling wild hogs and nearly getting yourself killed? What in the hell is wrong with you? If you had been killed we would have lost the war right then."

Adrian suddenly felt like a school child being dressed down by the principal. His anger flared but he remained outwardly calm and cool. "I still have to feed my family you know. Certainly the tree limb breaking was unanticipated and presented certain complications. But events like that are fairly rare."

"Fairly rare?" The Admiral echoed with overt sarcasm, showing how concerned he was. "'Fairly rare' is too damn often, Adrian. You must stop taking needles risks. You're too important to too many people. It's not as though we have anyone qualified waiting in the wings to pick up where you leave off. Look, I'll make a deal with you. I'll assign a hunter to provide all the food your family needs until the war is over. I'll assign twenty hunters if need be. I'll personally make sure your family is always supplied with food and whatever else they might need so that you can stop taking these ungodly risks. Deal?"

"Our Constitution forbids that, Admiral."

"Adrian, we are in a state of war, a state of emergency. I'm sure the Constitution has some provision for feeding the Commander in Chief's family during times such as these. If not, then let's call the Congress together and make an amendment."

Adrian paused for a long moment. "Okay, you win. I'll bow to this, but only until the war is over."

Both Linda and the Admiral were extremely relieved to hear Adrian capitulate. But Adrian was unhappy with the decision; he had just lost his one small diversion from the huge burden he was carrying. "Tell you what Admiral, how about if you take back the surplus of pork I seem to have accumulated, and on your next trip bring back an equal weight of shrimp. I haven't had shrimp in ages."

Fears about Adrian's hunting addressed, the Admiral then moved onto the subject of his visit: the friend or foe identification system. "It's called IFF for Identify Friend or Foe. In WWII a system was devised using transponder signals that's simple enough we can re-create it without difficulty. Basically the first ship sends a coded signal to the second ship. The second ship's transponder automatically shifts to a different frequency and sends back a coded signal. This system has the positive ability to identify friends, but that does not automatically mean that a ship not responding correctly is an enemy. There could be equipment malfunction, atmospheric anomalies, or a friendly could be using the wrong code. Still, it gives a high probability of identifying friends from foes and no system we can devise at this point is going to do any better."

"Speed is the key here; can we fit the ships in time? Can we make enough of them?" Adrian asked.

"Yes and yes." The Admiral replied. "We're already building them in several locations. They aren't technically difficult for our trained technicians to make. We'll have them on the ships in time – just barely in time mind you – but in time. We've also set up a ship-to-shore coded communications system so that we can keep track of all of our boats, know where they are, and collate the information they send back to us. That way our boats won't be out just searching at random and randomly coming across each other. We've assigned them in squadrons of three boats. We're thinking that's the optimal hunting pack number for this operation.

"As conditions warrant, the squadrons can come together when and if a large fleet of enemy ships is located. Each squadron will be assigned a specific search area to operate within, but be flexible enough to move to other areas as target opportunities arise. And, as you suggested, our attack subs will be patrolling on the front edge of the suspected travel paths of the Chinese. The CME took out our fixed sonar detection system, losing both cable and satellite communications. But we still have the towed arrays that can be deployed by our submarines. That gives us the capability of detecting, while remaining undetected ourselves, any shipping that comes through the patrolled areas. The subs will direct our attack boats in on the Chinese boats."

"Have you found any signs of the Chinese flotillas yet?" Adrian asked.

"Not yet, but if your predictions are accurate it should be any day now; and, of course, we expect the first signs to be directly from the west."

"What's our operational capability right now?"

"Eighty percent. We can launch eighty percent of what we think we can put together. Every day we gain another percent. We can put up a hell of a fight right now, but we really need that other twenty percent." The Admiral replied.

"Let's hope we get another twenty days then, but I'm not counting on it." Adrian said.

CHAPTER 9

AT DAWN THE NEXT MORNING, as Adrian was cooking breakfast, the Admiral pounded on Adrian's door. "Come on in Admiral" Adrian said. "From the look on your face, I'm guessing we've spotted the first fleet coming from China."

"We have, and they have several hundred ships coming at us. Probably more than that, but that's what we can detect right now. ETA in the Hawaii area is three days, tops."

Adrian calmly said, "I'll wake Linda and we can all eat breakfast. Then we'll fire up the chopper, go to Corpus and get a lift to Hawaii. You and I are going to be at the front line when this first battle goes down."

Two and a half days later, Adrian and the Admiral were at Pearl Harbor boarding a Navy cruiser. As soon as they were on board the ship shoved off and headed for the enemy fleet. They would soon catch up to the explosive boat carriers that had launched two days before. The cruiser could easily attain thirty knots and was highly maneuverable.

"How soon will we be in range of the enemy Admiral?" Adrian asked. He was already a little queasy from the rolling of the ship. Adrian always got seasick, he'd had the experience more than once.

"A day-and-a-half to two days Adrian. You look a little green." The Admiral said with a small smile. "Don't tell me you're going to have to carry a bucket around with you? Need some pills?"

"I'm sure I'll provide plenty of amusement for you and the crew. I always get seasick and it never gets better with time either. No pills though, they don't help and make me sleepy. And yeah, I'll probably be needing a bucket pretty soon."

"Let me take you on a tour of the boat and then show you to your quarters. You might as well lie low until we get closer." With that the Admiral took Adrian for an extended tour of the ship, showing him everything from the engine room to the control room. "This" said the Admiral "is the control room, this is where we'll be for most of this voyage. This is the heart of the combat operations."

Adrian looked around at what to him was a smallish and crowded room. All of the walls were lined with instruments and large panels. The room was shrouded in soft blue light with the instruments lit up with their own individual lights. It was a meaningless and complicated array to Adrian. He knew that every single instrument meant something important to the men operating the room, but they were Greek to him. In the center of the room was a waist-high panel with a large round nearly horizontal display surrounded by toggles and switches. On the round display were various symbols. To Adrian this appeared to show ships' locations in relation to each other, a kind of living map.

"Admiral, this is no doubt where you need to be, but I'll just be in the way; I'm already afraid to be in here. I have no doubt that I'll end up puking on something important, and I can't tell hide from hair on what I'm seeing. I'll be up on the bridge where I can see and be in communication with you. I'll have a bit more room for my bucket up there."

"As you wish, Mr. President."

Adrian laughed, "I know you don't approve, but trust me on this. You don't want me down here getting in your way. I'll know as much as I need to from your reports. We'll both be a lot happier if I am not under your feet in here. When the time comes to start sinking the Chinese ships, I want to be out there in one of the helicopters to see the engagement with my own eyes anyway. I need to see how the explosive boats work out in real time."

"We've had this conversation, Adrian," the Admiral said with a grave tone. "It's extremely risky. The helicopters are too vulnerable."

"You're going to send at least one out anyway to get a visual report, aren't you?" Adrian asked.

"Of course. But losing a helicopter and crew isn't on the same level as losing our Commander In Chief! Jesus, Adrian, how many times do we have to talk about this?"

"Look Admiral" Adrian replied with sudden steel in his voice. "I won't lead from behind. I need to see the action for myself, see if there are problems or improvements to be made. I can't do that sitting and watching radar screens. I won't stay out there for the whole battle, but I have to be out there at the beginning of it in case I see something I haven't considered. I need to know what the actual work of this operation looks like, how fast the boats can move and turn, what positions they're best arrayed in. For ninety-eight percent of this war I'll be out of harm's way – after all, I can't be everywhere at once. But in order to understand *what* needs to be done and *how* it needs to be done, I have to see this for myself. It's also good for the morale of the fighting sailors to know they're leader isn't afraid to mix it up. They deserve the respect of a leader who takes the risks they're taking. When it gets hard and tight out there, I want every sailor on every boat we have to know I am in that helicopter out in front of them. I want them to know they're not sacrificial lambs. Remember Admiral, these are not naval warriors going out on the front line, their expertise isn't combat, it was commerce. They don't have the fighting background – they'll need all the encouragement they can get."

As the helicopter lifted off, Adrian was immediately relieved of the sea sickness he'd been suffering since boarding the cruiser. Flying didn't bother him in the least, even though the helicopter flight had more motion in more directions than the cruiser had. Moments after the naval chopper had reached altitude Adrian could see the layout of the explosive boat carriers, and only a mile away he saw the fleet of oil tankers. Between the two fleets he could see dozens of small boats moving rapidly towards the tankers. The war had started.

"Fly over close to the tankers, I want to get a look at them up close." Adrian instructed the pilot.

"How close do you want to get sir?"

"Close enough to make out faces."

"Yes sir, I'll get you close enough to count pimples." And so he did. Within minutes the chopper was circling around the foremost tanker close enough to clearly see startled faces. When several soldiers suddenly popped up on deck and began firing at the chopper with rifles the pilot calmly asked "Close enough sir?" He smiled. A bullet snipped through the aluminum skin on the chopper making a loud ping, punctuating his question.

"Yep, I think that will do, go ahead and back off a bit, son. And move around to the stern of this boat, I want a good look at the rudder."

Adrian flipped a switch on the radio and was then able to broadcast to the American fleet on an open frequency. "Captains, I've been looking at the rudders of a couple of these ships. Because the ships are not carrying the weight they were designed for, they are riding high in the water. As the waves recede from below the stern, part of the rudder is temporarily exposed, and the propellers are near the surface. If you bring your torpedo boats around from behind and time the hit with the waves you may be able to disable their rudders, possibly even damage the props.

"From directly behind though, the rudders will be a difficult target to hit, but if you come at them from the side you stand a better chance. Disabling their ability to steer is as good as, or maybe better than, sinking them. If we're lucky, other ships will come to the rescue of a disabled ship to off-load their soldiers. On the other hand they may just sail on by; in either case a rudderless ship isn't a threat to us."

"If you can't get to the rudder you'll have to try and breach the hull. Most of these tankers have double hulls. To sink one, you'll have to not only flood the inner hull, but at least two of the inner tanks.

"That means that you'll have to breach the outer hull and then run another boat in through that breach to hit the inner hull and tank in at least two separate places, say about at quarter points along the length of the ship. Now, let's see what you can do to their rudders."

Adrian watched closely as the first of the radio-controlled explosive packed boats rapidly approached the foremost tanker. The little boat looked like a mosquito next to an elephant. For the first time Adrian had deep doubts about the effectiveness of his strategy. It didn't seem possible that his tiny little boats could even cause a paint chip on the behemoths, much less stop or sink them.

As the tiny craft approached he saw men with small arms swarm the deck. He watched as the soldiers fired on the approaching boat with rifles and rocket propelled grenades. The water was pocked around the boat from the rifle bullets. The two RPGs missed by yards. Adrian held his breath – if one of those bullets hit the boat in the right place, the whole thing would go up prematurely.

The closer the boat came, the more bullets poured into it, but the outboard engines had been shielded, and the boat kept on. Finally the little boat was nearly to the stern of the big ship and made a sudden turn towards it. The little boat disappeared momentarily beneath the behemoth's bulk and then there was a large gout of flames. The shock wave could be seen spreading across the ocean's surface for a hundred yards.

For several long moments it appeared that the explosion had had no impact on the ship's operation. But slowly it began to lose speed and then coasted to a sudden stop. Adrian had the pilot bring the chopper in directly behind the tanker, come up close and then swerve off quickly taking defensive maneuvers to avoid the small arms fire.

Adrian flipped the broadcast switch again and announced, "The first tanker is stopped dead in the water, rudder is in shreds and I think the propeller was damaged as well. Great shooting whoever that was!" Adrian could hear cheering from open mikes aboard several of the ships in the fleet. "Now go get them!" Adrian shouted. He looked down and saw scores and scores of the small boats making their way towards the fleet of giant ships.

"Sir, we've taken a hit to the hydraulics and have to return to the cruiser immediately. We may not make it all the way." The pilot said to Adrian with no more stress in his voice than if he was ordering a ham sandwich.

"Well, get us as close as you can." The pilot was able to get them within a quarter mile of the cruiser. He made a good landing, shutting off the rotors in time to keep them from becoming shrapnel when they hit the water. They bailed out and were floating in their life preservers while waiting to be picked up.

Adrian wiped seawater from his eyes, then looked at the pilot and said "Sorry about that. We wouldn't have lost the chopper if I hadn't ordered you to fly in close. I'll tell the Admiral you did a top-notch job of flying and that it was strictly my fault. And that *was* top notch flying, the very best."

The pilot smiled and said , "I'd be proud to be your pilot anytime and anywhere, sir. I haven't had that much fun since I first started flying. Damn, but what a story this will make, I've got bragging rights for the rest of my life – thank you sir, thank you very much!"

Adrian smiled and shook his head. *How can we lose with men like this on our side?*

CHAPTER 10

RACE HAD COMPLETED HER ROUNDS of ham operators and then been assigned to escort duty for groups of volunteers moving supplies to Corpus Christi for the war effort. In Adrian's absence, Linda, the commander of the Fort Brazos Militia, had also taken command of the Texas Rangers. This particular group that Race was escorting had located hundreds of artillery shells in the warehouses at Fort Hood. These shells were carefully stored in eighteen-wheeler trucks that other volunteers had been gathering and returning to operating condition. Race was continually amazed at the scope and breadth of the war effort, and how many Texans had turned out to volunteer. She knew that operations like this were taking place all across the country.

On a previous escort mission, she had gathered a group of Rangers and Militia to guard a tanker truck of diesel fuel from Corpus Christi to Fort Hood, to fill the trucks that would be carrying the artillery rounds back. She couldn't see how artillery rounds would be useful to raiders, but then raiders didn't always act with logic – and wouldn't know the trucks cargo anyway. Raiders spying trucks moving cross country with an armed escort would assume that the contents of the trucks were worth stealing, whatever the contents might be, and would definitely want a tanker. So Race kept a sharp look-out for trouble.

It was a three-day trip, mainly because Race wouldn't allow the convoy to travel after dark. Darkness made a road ambush of the convoy an almost certainty. Instead she picked out a wide open area each evening and had the trucks parked. If they came under fire, being near trucks filled with artillery and diesel wasn't where she wanted to be. Instead she had the drivers and passengers camp nearby, and mounted a constant patrol around the vehicles. There was no campfire, and no smoking allowed. They kept a dark camp and a quiet camp. Every man and woman with the trucks was armed and participated. All together they were a formidable force to contend with.

The second evening out, they came under attack. Race was patrolling to the south side of the parked trucks when she heard a rifle shot from the west side. The convoy's people knew what to do; they had drilled on this several times. The perimeter guards were scattered out fairly thinly, their job wasn't to mount a counter-attack, but to alert the reserve contingent to danger. Half of the reserve contingent would rush to where the action appeared to be – the other half waited where they were in case the first action was a diversion.

This one was a diversion. Each guard remained where they were. Race rushed towards where the gunshot had come from. Before she got there she heard three more shots. She joined the reserves as she arrived, all of them taking cover.

Race quickly warned everyone to be ready to move, this was possibly just a distraction so that the attackers could surprise them from a different spot. She then trotted over to the rest of the reserves just as rapid shots were fired from the east. She led the reserves to that point, and found three of the guards in a heated fire fight with an unknown number of attackers.

Assessing the situation, Race sent a runner to bring over half of the other reserves, leaving half where they were just in case. When the rest of them arrived, she gave quick instructions to spread out, find cover, and fire at anything suspicious outside of the line. Five minutes later there came a rush of feet and rapid gunfire from multiple locations. The defenders returned fire. The shooting was over in less than two minutes, with the attacker's fire petering out to nothing. Race suspected that a small group of raiders had attacked, taken too much fire to suit them, and retreated. She didn't think they would be back.

With the morning sun up Race scouted the area of the action. She found one dead man and a wounded boy, about fifteen with a through and through leg wound that Race cleaned and bandaged while she questioned him.

The boy, seeing that Race had no intention of hurting him, and was in fact solicitous of his wound, was a bit smitten, and talked freely.

He described the band he had been with as ten men and three teenage boys. They had seen the trucks after pulling over for the evening and hadn't realized how many defenders there were, or how well armed.

They thought that truck drivers would be easy to take. They had discounted the escort vehicles when they realized the occupants were mostly female. He said, "They'll be miles away by now, afraid of being trailed and attacked. They figured out at the last minute that those women were Rangers and know they stirred up a hornet's nest. They won't be back."

"What about you?" Race asked. "Are you going to join up with them again?"

"No way. The bastards left me here to die. I was about to quit them anyway, taking from people turns out to be something I didn't feel good about. I just want to go home and do my best at farming. I've had enough of the outlaw life. Besides, the Rangers are catching and killing more and more outlaws every day, it's gotten to be a damned dangerous business to be in."

Race and the boy talked on about things in general when something the boy said got her full attention. She was finishing up the bandage and getting ready to move the trucks out when he said "We traded with some Chinese men a few days back, down south of here a ways. They were too well-armed for us to try to take them, but they gave us food just for information."

"Tell me all about this." Race said with barely a show of interest, although she was on high alert inside.

"Well...it must've been two weeks ago. We stumble-bumped into them on accident. It was a bit scary there for a few minutes, all of them armed and pointing military weapons at us, and all of us exposed and pointing military weapons at them. If anyone fired a shot, most everyone was going to die right there. Their leader and ours shouted at each other for a while, then calmed down and started to just talk. Man it was intense though, everyone on edge like that.

"Then this guy offered us food for information. That turned the trick and everyone settled down."

"What did they want to know?" Race asked.

"It seems silly but they just wanted to know about the conditions from San Antonio to Lubbock. Said they were going that way to find some friends in Lubbock and wanted to know about traveling conditions, how many people along the route, that sort of thing."

"How many were there, how were they dressed, what kind of guns did they have?"

"There were ten of them, in regular clothes like everyone else, with rifles that looked kind of like a bull-pup assault rifle. They gave us food... kind of like MRE's... only they had weird food in them. One of the foods was a pickled root-like thing. Not bad, but weird."

"Did they all speak English?"

"Couldn't say for sure, only the head guy did any talking. But he gave orders in English and they seemed to understand him well enough. Told them to lower their rifles, then later for each man to get out one ration pack. After a bit we left, walking backwards, and they watched us go. That was kind of scary, too, 'cause they might have changed their minds. Still, it would have been a bloody business for them as well."

"Where did you bump into them? I mean tell me

exactly where." Race said. The boy looked at her hard now, realizing for the first time that this was more than just a casual conversation. He explained where, giving her landmarks that she could easily find.

Race continued to question the boy, but didn't learn anything else interesting. She said, "Look kid. I've patched you up and letting you go. But it's only because I have other things to do right now. When I'm back on patrol, I better not find you raiding again, because I'll kill you if I do."

"Yes Ma'am, I mean, no Ma'am. I'm done with that I promise."

Race mulled over the boy's story. Later that morning after they were back on the road, Race called Corpus Christi on the encrypted radio, asked for the intelligence office, and then relayed the story. "Pass it along to President Hunter, too." She said. "This sounds like a recon patrol; but of what I can't figure out. Maybe he'll know."

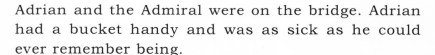

Adrian and the Admiral were on the bridge. Adrian had a bucket handy and was as sick as he could ever remember being.

"Adrian, why don't we send you back to land now? You look like hell and you have to feel worse than you look."

"Soon Admiral. I want to see this particular action finished. We're learning a lot as we go and I want to be right here to learn it. The Chinese figured out that they could use tracer rounds to blow up the explosive boats damn fast. Switching to night operations has helped, but we've now got to get all of our torpedo boats fitted with infra-red cameras. These guys are smart and adapt rapidly. I need to see what they'll come up with next. I intend to stay until we've come up with a method of destroying them that they can't counter."

The Admiral nodded. "Thought you'd say something like that," he mumbled

"What was that Admiral? You were mumbling."

"I said, what did you make of Race's report?"

Adrian smiled; he'd heard what the Admiral said. The smile made Adrian look even more ghastly than he already did, his white teeth contrasting with his green pallor. "It's damned odd. She's right, it sounds just like a recon... but of what? There's nothing out there but mesquite and rattlesnakes. Lubbock doesn't have anything of military value."

"Let's assume that it's a Chinese Army recon. How did they get where they are?" the Admiral asked.

"My guess is through Mexico. They could have landed anywhere along Mexico's east coast and walked in. No problem really. But *how* isn't nearly as interesting as *why*. I've been racking my brains, and can't come up with any reason for it – but it isn't just something random, they have a reason... and it will be a damn good reason, too. We need to know what that reason is. Which means we have to capture and interrogate the patrol."

"Hell, Adrian, they could be anywhere out there. How in the world are you going to find them?"

"Admiral, they're not just anywhere out there. We have a specific location for them as of two weeks ago. And, if they didn't use Lubbock as a diversion – which maybe they did – then we know where they're going. They are somewhere between those two points, closer to Lubbock by two weeks. That gives us a fairly specific area to look in. I've already sent orders for Race to put together a hunting party. She'll find them, she's damn good at hunting men. I also ordered a special ops team to be on standby and ready to chopper in when she locates them."

Adrian turned his back to the Admiral and retched into the bucket, then turned back. "From the sound of it they'll be special ops soldiers. Well trained, skilled, and well-armed. They won't be captured easily, it'll take a team better trained and better skilled to do that. I've explained that to Race...I have confidence she'll find them, but I'm worried that she may exceed her orders and try to capture them. Trouble is we need them alive...and Race...well Race has more experience at killing than capturing."

CHAPTER 11

ADRIAN WAS IMMENSELY RELIEVED WHEN he finally returned to the solid, unmoving land at Pearl Harbor. The seasickness faded within minutes of disembarkation. For the time being, the war was in the Pacific and he wanted to stay close, make occasional fly-overs to see the action for himself. This was largely a time of experimentation and adaptation of the strategy he had envisioned, and so far it was working well. Getting the small boats rigged with infra-red had allowed them to attack under cover of darkness, yet it was still less accurate than attacking during the day. He was trying to figure out a way they could attack during the day.

Adrian was talking to one of the engine mechanics, an older man named Ray. Ray was a long time mechanic, his fingernails permanently stained black underneath. "Ray, is there some kind of shielding we could put over the explosives? I know it would be heavy but could it work?"

"Naw, I don't think so. They're blowing these things up as fast as we can get them out there. Adding another level of scrounging materials and fabrication would slow us way down. Besides, those fellas are going to shoot holes through anything light enough for the boats to handle."

"Well I'm stumped then." Adrian admitted. "I can't think of anything that's going to let us work during the day."

"You know...maybe it isn't the boats that's the problem. Maybe it's how you're using em."

"What do you mean?" Adrian asked.

"Maybe you need to swarm the tankers with a whole bunch of boats at the same time, give them too many targets to be able to focus on effectively. When one of them gets through and does its damage, you can bring the rest of em back, or send 'em on to the next target. Kind of like a swarm of mosquitoes. You can slap at one or two mosquitoes pretty easily, but when there's a swarm, they'll drive you crazy as a shit-house rat."

Ray watched Adrian's face as he said this. He noted that his worry lines smoothed out slightly and that his eyes, while wide open, had lost their focus. Adrian was visualizing the approach Ray had suggested and slowly a small smile crept across his face. Suddenly Adrian's eyes were aware of Ray again with a concerted stare.

"Ray you're a genius! It's so simple that I feel like I should slap my own face for not thinking of it. Man you may have just changed the entire war, and in our favor. Thank you!" Adrian jumped up and strode off quickly, muttering to himself with every step. Ray watched him go, shook his head a few times, and then returned to the job at hand.

"Damn it Adrian," said the Admiral. "We're barely keeping up with boat manufacturing as it is, and now you want us to have twenty times as many?"

"No, you're not seeing it right. Look at it this

way. Instead of attacking ten tankers at a time with two boats on each tanker, we attack one tanker with twenty boats. As soon as the target is disabled, the remaining boats move on to the next tanker and so on. It's the same number of boats. In fact, we'll probably lose fewer boats in the process because each tanker's defenders will have too many boats to focus on. In the long run we may stop more tankers with fewer boats. The only downside is fuel capacity for the boats. Each boat will be out longer, burning more fuel. We may have to bring them back periodically for refueling."

"Or..." the Admiral mused "...fit them with additional fuel tanks."

Adrian stared at the Admiral for a few seconds. "Seems like I just keep missing the obvious doesn't it?" Adrian stood up and looked out the second story window, not seeing anything because his mind was inwardly focused.

"Not at all, Adrian. You're just learning to use the minds of other people to get to the results you have already decided need to be gotten. Look, command leadership isn't about being the smartest person in the room. It's about using all the resources you can find, especially other people's ideas, and then making the right things happen. You provide the overall strategy, the intermediate and long range goals, and the motivation. You sift through all the ideas you can find, determine which ones will work the best, then implement those actions through the efforts of others. You motivate people to want to be involved in making these goals happen. You direct their efforts in the best pattern because you see how it all fits together, and necessarily each of them is focused only on the details of their particular part in the overall mission."

Adrian turned from the window to look at the Admiral as he continued, "You're learning the reality of being in charge of a very large operation, an operation spread across an entire country. A commander understands that it's not about him, it's about getting the job done in the best way possible and it does not matter who comes up with the best ideas. You have a natural instinct for this. If you had been wrapped up in your own ego you would never have talked to the right person who had the right idea at the right time. He knew you were really listening to him, and he gave you his best thoughts, as no doubt he is giving you his best efforts every day."

Now the Admiral was standing. "Can you imagine Bonaparte sitting down with a private and discussing tactics? No, never. But if he had, he might have found another way to fight, a better way. Great ideas often come from surprising places, and if you're not open-minded about hearing them, you hinder yourself. So, by having an open mind you have come up with two new ideas and different tactics to use in your overall strategy. Don't beat yourself up, Adrian, you're doing just fine. You're doing it right. You're the one who discovered these ideas, even though they didn't come from inside your own head."

Adrian was slightly embarrassed. He felt a strong affection for the Admiral, and it was obvious to him that the Admiral returned the feeling. The Admiral was doing an excellent job of mentoring Adrian, a fact Adrian had only recently become aware of.

With the Admirals help and frankness, Adrian was slowly growing into the position he had reluctantly taken on.

To cover this sudden rush of emotion, Adrian did the typical male thing – changed the subject. "Any news yet from the Atlantic side?"

The Admiral was just as happy to be on a different topic, for the same reasons as Adrian. "Not yet. It seems they're in a holding pattern. My guess is that they still think they'll sneak up on us on the East Coast. But every day that they delay is another day of preparation for us. Using the tactics we're perfecting here, we'll wallop them when they finally show up."

As soon as Race had seen the trucks into Corpus Christi, she received her new orders. Find the Chinese recon team, keep an eye on them, and call in a Seal team from Corpus. Race had mixed emotions about this. When she found the recon team she wanted to lead the team that captured them. She knew in her heart she could do it, and do it well. But she had also learned to obey orders. Adrian had driven that point home very effectively when she and the girls had taken off from Corpus Christi to join up with Adrian in the war with Mexico. She had disobeyed Adrian's orders, and he had been savagely brutal in pointing that fact out, and what the repercussions to the war effort could have been. He had been just as savage and brutal in his assessment of her behavior and pulled no punches in telling her just how badly she had fouled up, and how she had damaged his trust in her. Race wasn't going to deliberately disobey Adrian's orders ever again, but she would be ready in case circumstances changed.

Race picked two other rangers to accompany her on the mission to find the recon unit. She was under temporary command of the Seal team leader for this search and find operation, and he questioned her on her decision to use a three-person team. "Why three? I can send as many as twenty with you, well trained and well-armed."

"Twenty, Robert?" Race didn't stand on protocol when addressing the military. "Twenty people bumbling around the countryside? Can't you imagine what a fiasco that would be? Look, my mission is simple – find the recon team and report back to you on their location. Finding them means guessing about where they are now and going there, looking around and asking questions. Ten Chinese men are going to be noticed. Possibly noticed often, unless they are only moving at night. Truth is I'd rather go alone, but I'm being nice to you by taking two Rangers with me. All I need is food, water, an encrypted radio, a map that's a twin of one you have, and a helicopter ride."

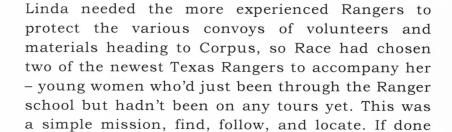

Linda needed the more experienced Rangers to protect the various convoys of volunteers and materials heading to Corpus, so Race had chosen two of the newest Texas Rangers to accompany her – young women who'd just been through the Ranger school but hadn't been on any tours yet. This was a simple mission, find, follow, and locate. If done properly, there wouldn't be any fighting. It would be good training for them and she could keep a close eye on their every move. She really would have preferred to be on her own for this, but she'd said she would take two Rangers with her, and now she had to. She'd just make the best of the situation and get in some solid training time with the two newbies.

Joan was twenty, quiet and thoughtful; athletic and tall, with close-cropped blonde hair. Ruth was nineteen, short and muscular for a woman. She had long black hair and fire in her belly – she wasn't afraid of anything at any time. That fearlessness worried Race; it was something she wanted to keep an eye on and help her learn to control, if possible. She thought the two girls would make a good team, each adding positive attributes the other lacked.

The chopper set them down a mile outside the city of Junction. Race had spent a full day looking at the map, thinking about where the boy had said he'd seen the Chinese men, working out how she would get to Lubbock from there, and gauging how far they would have traveled by now. She thought they would be further up than Junction but she didn't want to overshoot them. She needed to find their trail so, she decided to land behind where she thought they might be, question everyone they came across, and hopefully strike their trail that way. If she landed ahead of them she would never find them. It was a guessing game – one she was afraid of over-thinking. Finally she sighed, put her finger on Junction on the Texas map and said out loud "Here." And there they were, getting off the helicopter and watching it quickly disappear, leaving them in the semi-desert surrounded by stunted mesquite trees. Race had them landed about as far out of town as she thought the Chinese might have avoided the town by. Now the work began.

Race drew a rough sketch in the dirt for the two girls to look at. "We're here." She said placing a pebble on the sketch. "I think they're about here." Race sketched out an oval area to the Northwest three days march ahead of them, straddling Highway 277. "More or less anyway. What we're going to do is to zigzag back and forth across an area one mile wide on each side of the highway, looking for people to question. If they're forward scouts for an invading force, that force is going to be mechanized and will stay on the paved roads, so we'll be staying close to the road. I still can't imagine what's in Lubbock they'd be interested in, but it's all we have to go on."

Race stood, stretching for a moment to get out the kinks from the helicopter ride, and wiped her face with a bandana. The heat was oppressive. She didn't notice the slight smell of the mesquites as she took a sip of warm water from her canteen.

"When we find traces of their passing, which will almost surely be from eye-witnesses, then we'll be able to line out and move faster. I expect we'll actually catch up to them somewhere around here." Race squatted again and scratched another oval surrounding San Angelo. "This is rough, dry country and we have to move fast. It's going to be short rations, water restriction and little sleep. In other words, it's going to be damned hard and there is no going back. We won't get a chopper to come pick anyone up. If you break a leg out here you're going to be in serious trouble... so be damn careful. Any questions?"

Joan and Ruth shook their heads, mouths set in similar, grim lines.

"Okay, let's go." Race picked up her backpack and, shouldering into the straps, started walking, looking for the nearest habitation. She swept the ground with her eyes as she walked.

You never know, it's always possible to actually cross their trail.

CHAPTER 12

FOR THREE DAYS RACE, JOAN, and Ruth walked across the harsh country, cutting back and forth across Highway 277, talking to at least a dozen people before they found anything of interest.

They'd stopped at a farm and talked to the farmer and his wife. "Just yesterday I was talking to Tom and he told me he'd seen some armed men off in the distance – maybe four or five days ago from the way he talked. You might want to talk to Tom...he lives about five miles that way, old house next to a large granite escarpment." The farmer pointed to the west.

Two hours later they found Tom. "Sure, I seen em," he said. "Ten of 'em, I counted. Didn't like their looks, so I stayed hid. They was about a hunnert yards off. Quiet and sneaky like. Come on I'll show you." He led them back behind his house a half a mile and pointed out where he had been, down in a dry wash under some salt cedars. "Right over there." He pointed.

They walked to the spot he pointed to and found the tracks. Military-style boot prints were still visible, but wind-blown and blurry. "How long ago exactly?" Race asked with a hint of excitement.

"Four days. Was 'bout noon."

Race thanked the man and immediately she, Ruth, and Joan started following the tracks. They were easy enough to follow most of the time, generally staying parallel to Highway 277 and staying fairly close to it.

"Look." Race said when they found their campsite. "They've cleaned up. No trash and they buried the ashes from their fire. If you didn't know to look, you'd never notice a thing. Probably from habit, since I don't think they expect to be followed. They haven't completely hidden themselves from sight and they're traveling in daylight, so they must think no one is on to them."

Ruth said, "How are we going to catch up with them? It takes us longer to work out their tracks than it does for them to make them. We're falling farther behind every hour."

Race replied. "We're going to get some wheels and drive up 277. We'll stop every now and then and check for tracks. They've been tracking Highway 277 since we found them, so I expect they'll continue like this until they get to San Angelo, then they'll follow along Highway 208 to Colorado City. We'll find them on 208, before Colorado City, I think."

Joan rubbed her short hair and looked around at the desolate country. "Where are we going to get wheels, Race?"

"There must be some around here somewhere. These ranches are remote, they have to have transportation of some kind – at least some of them will. Once we find some, we can talk to the owners. When they understand it's part of the war effort – if they've heard of the war – I think we can get a loan."

They stopped at three ranches with no luck, but at the third they were given a tip about a man who had a truck and went on to the fourth ranch house It was occupied by an old man who was clearly surprised to see three young women armed with assault rifles approaching his house. "Y'all hold up right there and keep your hands where I can see them," the old man hollered from a window. A rifle barrel poked from the windows, but the man himself was not visible.

"We're Texas Rangers and we're on a war-effort mission sir," Race shouted back.

"Come on up slowly, but keep those hands in sight," he yelled back.

They approached slowly, careful with their hands, their rifles slung over their shoulders. The old man had moved to the doorway, rifle at the ready. "Rangers eh? Well they ain't making Rangers like they used to, that's for sure. Show me some ID."

The three women complied, showing their badges. The old man said, "Well hell, those badges don't mean nothin'. Anyone could make a badge like that. But I believe you anyway. I've heard tell of women Rangers and no one would make up a damn fool story like that. Ya'll come on in out of the sun, sit a spell and tell me what you want." He turned and walked into the house.

"At war with China eh? Damn shenanigans that's what that is. Well girls, this is your lucky day. I got a 1950 Chevy pickup truck in the barn. Still runs like a top. My son bought her and fixed her up real nice. He drove her occasionally before he was killed. I start her up once in a while to keep the battery fresh, drive her a mile or so every month to work the moving parts a bit. Got plenty of gasoline in the tank. I'll let you take her if you promise to bring her back as good as she is now. She ain't no speed wagon, got the original engine in her. But she'll cruise along at fifty miles per hour all day. Go much faster than that and it could be bad for her. Probably ain't another truck like that still running anywhere, damn sure ain't one around here. Fact is there's not much of nothing running around here these days. Everyone had those new computer cars, they all got burnt out by that solar storm."

As they drove off with the three of them crowded into the small cab, Race shook her head. "Can you believe he wrote out a receipt for me to sign? And always said 'her' instead of 'it.' Bet this truck has a name too, Sally, or Alice, or something. That's just plain funny."

The old man hadn't lied, the truck ran like a top. Every ten miles Race pulled over and they jumped out and looked for tracks. Knowing what they were looking for, it didn't take them long. The recon patrol had kept a consistent distance from the highway, always keeping it in sight, and they almost always stayed on the left side of it. As soon as they found tracks, the three Rangers would run back to the truck and take off again. After a while they stopped only after fifteen miles, and then only at twenty. When they started getting close to Colorado City they went back to checking every ten miles. The tracks were fresher now and Race was sure the patrol wasn't far ahead.

"Okay ladies." Race said as they got back into the

truck. "These tracks are fresh, no more than a day old. They still have crisp edges, the wind hasn't had time to erode them. We're changing our tactic. We're going to drive straight through to Colorado City at thirty miles per hour. You two ride in the back and watch the sides of the road very carefully. Keep your weapons out of sight and only your heads above the truck's sides. They'll hear us coming and take cover so don't look for men standing in the open. Watch all of the likely hiding places and look for men peeking out at us. If you see them don't let on, just pound on the cab after we're out of sight."

Moments before they reached the city limits Race pulled over. They all got out of the truck, rifles locked and loaded and slowly walked off the road. They searched thoroughly along both sides of the road, but found no sign of the recon patrol's tracks. Back at the truck Race leaned against the hot metal. "It looks like we've passed them, they aren't far back either. Okay, time to take a lookout position and call in."

Race looked the over country side, turning in a complete circle. "See that microwave tower? That's our spot." They clambered back into the truck and Race drove along FM 208 until they were near the tower. "We'll hide the truck and make a cold camp here. Come on let's move."

When the truck was hidden Race said, "I'm going to climb that tower, I should be hard to see because I'll blend into with those antennas. Give me the binoculars. You two rack out here until I come back, and remove the tail and brake lights... but save the bulbs to put back in. That old codger is sure to check."

Race walked to the tower and climbed over the surrounding fence. She climbed slowly, staying on the opposite side from where the recon patrol would be and climbing slowly to keep her motion from drawing the eye. When she got to the top she worked herself into a stable position behind one of the dish-like antennas and raised her binoculars and started scouring the other side of the highway. At their closest, the men would still be at least two miles away. They would have to be incredibly alert to spot her up on the tower. She barely moved and used binoculars with sun shades to prevent light from reflecting off the lenses.

Race watched and waited as the sun slowly sank off to her right. Her patience was finally rewarded an hour after dark when she saw a small pin-prick of a fire about four miles away. Race watched for a few minutes then climbed down and went back to the truck. Joan and Ruth were awake, eating cold rations.

"We've found them."

Race turned off the radio. "Okay, you heard them. The helicopters will meet us at the State Park north of here. They'll come in from the north, circling wide so there's no chance of being heard by the Chinese. Then we'll move south on foot to the ambush point and wait."

They got in the truck without slamming the doors, and Race took advantage of the teaching moment. "They may be four or five miles away, girls, but sound travels like the dickens after dark in this country.

We can use the headlights once we're pointed away from them." They reached the rendezvous point a half hour later. Race turned on the encrypted radio and they settled in to wait, taking turns at guard while the other two slept.

At four a.m. the radio squawked softly. Race picked it up and responded with the code reply. Ten minutes later she heard the choppers coming in; they were the stealth type and barely made any sound. Race signaled them in with a flashlight and the three helicopters settled into the open field, shutting down their rotors as they did so. After only a few minutes, a soldier appeared out of the darkness. He introduced himself as Frank, offered no rank. After they had talked for a moment Race unfolded her map. Using her flashlight she showed Frank where she suspected the recon patrol to be camped.

She then showed him where she thought the best ambush place to be. "See this field? It used to be plowed but it's gone to weeds. They're waist high and crowd right up to the road. There's no place a man can run without being seen. About all you can do is crawl through this stuff, and even that's going to move enough weeds to give you away. There's a dry river bed right here, a bridge on the paved road. That open field is going to funnel them up against the road where they can walk faster since they'll be exposed anyway. Any car coming will be heard miles away giving them plenty of time to take cover in the brush. When they get to the bridge they'll pause and listen real hard, then probably run across the bridge and then back to the edge of the road again."

She pointed to another spot on the map. "Right

here, at the other end of the bridge, there's a clump of old trees, mostly dead now, but still decent cover. If you put half of your men in those trees, they can block the bridge behind the patrol after they cross. Put men in the brush on this side of the bridge and when they get half-way across you'll have them in the wide open with nowhere to run or hide. We'll have them exposed with nowhere to go, no cover, and we probably won't have to fire a shot."

Frank nodded, "Okay Race, you've seen the terrain, we'll do it your way. Follow me, we'll brief the men and get moving; not much dark left."

CHAPTER 13

AS THE SUN BEGAN TO crease the horizon, the soldiers and the three Rangers had settled into their respective positions at each end of the bridge, Race and Frank where they could see the bridge and far down the road. If Race had calculated correctly, the Chinese recon patrol would be along in an hour, two at the most. She was tired, but excited. As the sun came up the temperature came up with it. Soon she was sweating. She took a sip from her canteen, her eyes never leaving the roadside where she expected them to appear. "Not to count chickens here, but what are the plans for these guys when we've got them?" Race asked Frank.

"Cuff them, call in the choppers, load them up, and take them back to Corpus Christi. There's a team of interrogators waiting."

"I can't go right back, I promised to return the pickup to the rancher I borrowed it from. Hell, he made me sign a receipt for it." Race chuckled again at the thought.

"Well now, if you signed a receipt then you definitely have to take it back. Hope you didn't tear it up too much, it's a classic. Wish I had one like it. You going to walk home after that?" Frank teased.

Race sighed, "Guess so. But you can drop Joan and Ruth off at Fort Brazos, can't you?"

Frank scratched at his scalp and grinned. "That's a bit out of the way, but maybe..."

The hours dragged on, past Race's estimate. Waiting was hot and boring. Race began having doubts, thinking maybe she had spotted someone else's camp fire. *Could have been hunters.* Another hour crawled by, seeming like a week to her instead of an hour.

Finally she saw movement where she had been staring for so long. A slight movement that wasn't immediately identifiable. She brought up her binoculars. She saw another movement that was mostly covered by brush, still not clearly a man. Suddenly a man emerged, then another, then eight more. The ten men were walking beside the road fairly casually.

"There they are! "Race said, unnecessarily since Frank was watching them, too.

Frank continued to watch through his binoculars and replied, "Yep, they fit the description alright. Now we just stay still until they're on the bridge. Let's hope they don't get cute and try to cross one at a time."

Shit! I hadn't thought of that. Race thought worriedly to herself.

She watched the Chinese through the heat waves as they drew closer, each minute slowly dragging by as she thought of all the possible things that could go wrong – and there were a lot of them. In spite of the slowness of their approach her heart was pounding. After what seemed like ages to Race, they arrived at the bridge approach and stopped for a brief conversation. They stood there for a full minute, apparently listening for any approaching vehicle. Then, on a signal from the lead man, they double-timed up and onto the bridge and began crossing it quickly.

When they reached the middle of the bridge the Seals on the far side emerged from hiding and took their positions behind them. They were visible, but had nearby cover, if needed. As soon as they were in place the team on Race's side of the bridge did the same. The Chinese men stopped and looked back and forth. Race thought they were about to put down their rifles, but was shocked at what happened next. They rapidly formed into an inwardly facing circle and began shooting each other. Within three seconds they were all down.

Stunned at what he had just witnessed, Frank said, "Well you were right, we didn't have to fire a shot. Let's see if any are still alive."

Race and Frank and two other men ran up onto the bridge. They moved forward rapidly, keeping the downed men under cover of their rifles, fingers on the triggers, removing weapons from each of the downed men as they came to them. Frank examined each of them, then suddenly yelled "Medic!" As two of Frank's men rushed up, Frank got on his radio and called the choppers to come in at maximum speed.

He said to Race, "Three are still alive, barely. We'll stabilize them best we can and rush them to the Fort Brazos hospital since it's closest. Maybe we can still get some information out of them. Maybe not, these men were damn sure dedicated to not being captured alive; getting them to talk might be impossible, assuming any of them live long enough to question."

The helicopters appeared within minutes, and the three wounded Chinese were loaded along with Joan and Ruth and several of the soldiers. The chopper lifted off and turned southeast and quickly faded out of sight. Frank saw to the loading of the second helicopter, putting as many of his soldiers on it as it could carry. It, too, took off and soon disappeared. That left Frank, Race, and five more soldiers for the third chopper. They dragged the bodies of the dead Chinese to the edge of the bridge and dumped them over the side.

Race said, "I'll walk back to the truck. Thank you, Frank, that was as well executed as it could have been. Even if we'd known they'd go suicide on us, there wasn't any way to prevent it. Tell Corpus Christi I'll radio in occasionally and let them know my progress."

Frank replied, "Hold on Race. We'll take you back to the truck, and then follow in a few hours to pick you up at the ranch. Show me on the map where it is." He studied the location Race pointed out for a minute, then looked up at her. "You know what?," he said. "I'll ride along with you, if you don't mind."

Race smiled, not trying to hide her pleasure at the idea. "Frank, you are the greatest!" She felt a stirring inside, a small feeling she never thought she would feel towards a man. Other than Adrian, she didn't trust men. She felt that she could trust Frank and was surprised at the feeling. Happily surprised.

The Admiral leaned over a large map of the world, showing Adrian where they had spotted and attacked

Chinese ships. "They learn quickly. They're adapting to our tactics by spreading as far apart as they can, putting miles of Pacific Ocean between their ships.. We've responded by spreading out as far as we can, too. We're going to miss a lot of them before they get in close to shore. We don't have the long-range, ocean-going vessels they have. But, once they get within range we'll find most of them, especially since they'll be heading towards the refineries and platforms."

Adrian thought for a moment, tapping his fingers on the table. "Spreading out slows down the number of ships we can stop, but it puts them in a bind, too. When they were closer together they could off-load their soldiers and weapons onto an undamaged ship. Now they won't be able to. The ships we don't sink will just drift, going where the currents and winds take them. By the time they get to land, if they ever do, they'll be starved and dehydrated. Shows how desperate they are – they're willing to sacrifice their troops without a hint of it bothering them. I wonder how that will affect their troop's motivation? Probably doesn't matter. Once they're out of the action they no longer count to us or to them. The rest will just keep on coming. And we'll just keep on stopping them. When they get closer, we'll be able to spot them from the air and direct our attack ships to them. It's going to get hot and heavy then. The closer-in they get, the more intense the action is going to become. The good news is that the longer it takes them to get close, the more boats we'll have ready and waiting."

Adrian stood up straight and began pacing

again, to the Admiral's annoyance. *Can't he ever just sit still?*

Adrian continued, "I expect the Atlantic attack won't come until we're fully engaged on the west coast. When they come in on the Atlantic side, they'll be spread out also, but they'll have the same problem, they'll have to concentrate again. They may land a few in places where there's no oil or refineries – places we don't expect them – off-load, and march to where their targets are, try to secure them for the incoming ships. We need to shape up the militias for those fights. It will be a numbers game as much as anything. One Chinese ship can easily carry two thousand soldiers. Get enough of those on land and our militias are going to be in for one hell of a fight."

The Admiral drew his finger across the map and stopped at Fort Brazos. "Only one of the Chinese recon soldiers made it to Fort Brazos alive, and he's in a coma. Our intelligence guys went through all the clothes and gear of their dead searching for a clue. Didn't find anything except the radio they used to report back. No maps, no documents of any kind. We still don't have a clue why they were scouting way out there in the boonies."

Adrian stopped pacing for a moment, "What're the chances he'll recover and be able to talk?"

"Fair. He's getting the best medical treatment we have. We're keeping him at Fort Brazos. Our guys have a plan for interrogating him. It's an old trick, but one that might work, given enough time. Since he was willing to commit suicide the chances of us getting him to talk are pretty slim, and even then we'll likely get some kind of misdirection. What we plan to do is to stage everything to look like he's been in a coma for a year. Post fake calendars all over the village, get every villager in on the act. He'll pretty much be given free rein to wander the village. He'll be treated as just another local and fed disinformation about the war having ended."

The Admiral stood, walked to the window and looked out, but kept talking.

"The goal is to convince him the war is over and his side lost. That the information he has is of no interest or value. He'll be taught English, if he doesn't already speak it – and we're betting they taught him that before sending him in. There'll be fake radio broadcasts and fake conversations intended for him to overhear."

The Admiral turned from the window to look at Adrian.

"This will take time as his wounds have to heal up sufficiently to fool him, and it's a bit risky in case someone slips and he figures it out. But, in the long run, the intelligence boys think they'll get accurate information faster. They're keeping him in an induced coma, only allowing him to regain consciousness for short periods. During those periods, he's being allowed to overhear rehearsed conversations that, if he understands them, sound like war gossip. By the time they allow him to wake fully, he'll have a set of buried memories that will make him think time has gone by and the war has ended, and his side lost. It's ambitious, but could prove out nicely."

Adrian replied, "The weak spots are how long it will take to get useful information, how you're going to convince him his wounds are healed when they aren't, and someone slipping and saying the wrong thing."

The Admiral said, "Yeah, I know. But those intelligence boys are clever. They're putting every possible medical technique to use, even keeping him in a hyperbaric chamber we had flown in. We've set up a high-tech laboratory on site. He's being treated with stem-cells, and his wounds are being attended to constantly by a plastic surgeon. On the surface, he will barely see any scar tissue. To him they'll look like year-old wounds that have healed nicely. They'll account for his weakness by telling him he's been unconscious and in bed for a year – he'll be twenty pounds heavier when he's allowed to 'come to'. They're also tube feeding him with high calorie formulas that will make him gain weight. He'll set a new Guinness record for fast healing, believe me. We're pulling out all the stops. The two Navy surgeons are actually breaking new ground here; it's like a research project for them."

The Admiral moved from the window and resumed his seat at the table. Adrian began pacing again.

The Admiral continued, "While he's sedated, he's being exposed to fake news reports of the war, as though time is truly passing. The psych boys say his subconscious will absorb the messages, and that will make him easier to convince. This is all being calibrated with the seasons and his recovery speed in mind so that he won't be suspicious of the time of year, season-wise, when he comes to. I almost feel sorry for him. Well not quite, but I wouldn't want to be in his shoes. The villagers are getting daily training in how to act around him, and being kept apprised of his progress. I'm told they're enjoying the hell out of it, especially the children. They're thinking he'll be more likely to believe young children than adults, and the kids think it's a hoot.

"The children have auditioned for the role of becoming his friend, taking him under their wing so to speak. Two of them, the winners of the audition, are being coached on how to become friends with him. All supervised of course, but from a distance. The effort going into this is tremendous."

Adrian replied, "I hope it pays off soon. Whatever they were scouting must be extremely important if they were willing to kill themselves to keep from revealing their mission. If it's that important to them, then it will be doubly important to us. Tell your intelligence group to hurry up every chance they get."

CHAPTER 14

ADRIAN WAS OFF ON ANOTHER F-16 tour, stopping often to meet with each militia and describe the possibility of Chinese forces landing and making their way to oil fields and refineries. In North Carolina the militia had gathered to hear him speak.

Adrian stood on an improvised platform and looked over the crowd. *These are some of the roughest and toughest men I've ever seen; mountain men, used to surviving in a hard world.* "We should be able to stop most, but not all, of the Chinese ships. But these tankers are huge. With just a little work they will have cleaned the tanks of oil reside, installed bunks, kitchens, and sanitary facilities. It is not an exaggeration to state that one tanker can carry two thousand Chinese soldiers. Trained infantry, special forces units, helicopters, tanks, weapons of every description. These are formidable opponents. They'll be disciplined and fearless. They'll be extremely well-armed and versed in the use of their weapons. They'll have armor on the ground and air cover. Stopping them will require specialized tactics; you won't have the resources they have, or the training.

"But, and this is a big but, they will have to move to where they want to get to. They won't be able to entrench and fight from a static position until they get there. This gives us an edge we can take advantage of, by using guerrilla-style hit-and-run techniques to wear them down, drain them by attrition. We're currently deploying stockpiles of surface to air missiles; you'll receive yours soon. You'll also receive portable anti-tank weapons you can use to strip them of their armor and air cover. We're gathering up mobile field artillery to distribute as well. Each militia will be given a short training on how to deploy, aim, and fire these. It'll be quick and elementary training, there isn't time to do full training. Same thing with mortars, anti-personnel mines, and heavy machine guns.

"You'll work out your own tactics; you know the terrain and where you can take best advantage of it. The overall strategy is to knock down their helicopters, then take out their armor, place anti-personnel mines in their path, hit them with artillery and mortars on a running basis, ambush them every chance you get. Mire them down, kill as many as of them as you can with the least number of losses you can manage. Keep at them day and night. Wear them out physically and mentally, don't let them get any sleep. Use your terrain against them. Force them into swamps or other areas they can't move through quickly. Eventually you'll stop their movement and they'll have to take a hard stand somewhere. Make it *your* choice where that is, then you have them.

"Once you get them to stop and fight, don't confront them in a frontal assault, just keep pounding them from a distance. Snipers will be especially effective in keeping their heads down while you pour it to them. At some point they may surrender. It'll be your choice to take prisoners or not, that's up to you."

Adrian paused to give them a moment to think.

"We don't know where or when they will make landfall, you'll need to set up a chain of coast watchers with runners or radios to let you know when ships are spotted. We've already set up locations for the transfer of armaments and training on them. We have damn little time, so make every minute count."

When the speech was finished, Adrian met with the local commanders and gave them the locations and estimated dates for the distribution of arms. Adrian couldn't meet with every militia, only some of them. He met with as many as he could, the rest were being briefed by other members of the military.

"Wake up sir! You're wanted on the radio," the pilot said on the intercom.

Adrian groaned, he had finally learned how to sleep in the F-16 trainer, and these naps were about the only sleep he had been able to get for days. Groggily he rubbed his face above the oxygen mask, then keyed the radio button. "Adrian here." He said into the mike.

"Adrian, the Chinese fleet in the Pacific has begun tightening into vectors aimed at the refineries. The action is picking up fast, and at this rate will be at high intensity within twenty-four hours. We've also started picking up signals of ships in the North Atlantic. The shit storm is brewing, and it's going to accelerate rapidly. I'd like you to return to Hawaii to help direct the battle." The Admiral's voice came across was clear, but he sounded strained.

"The West Coast side of the war doesn't need me as much as the East Coast side will, Admiral," replied Adrian. "I need to keep doing what I'm doing here – I still believe the main battle will be on this side. Put your best man in command and meet me in Corpus Christi in three days; I still have seven more stops to make."

"Yes Mr. President." Adrian couldn't tell if the Admiral was being polite or sarcastic. Either way, Adrian knew he was ultimately responsible and had to call the shots as he saw them.

"Good. I'll see you there in three days." Adrian switched off the radio and tried to go back to sleep, but remained wide awake.

Adrian completed his cross-country tour and was back in Corpus Christi, meeting with the Admiral on the aircraft carrier.

"I'm going home for a few days. I think it may be the last time I'll be able to see Linda for several months. I plan to move from hotspot to hotspot to help as much as I can. I want a communications unit to go with me, to send and receive full communications and hourly updates. Admiral, you have charge of the West Coast war. You know the drill and can get our assets into place faster than anyone else. I'll bounce around as needed. Don't get caught up in worrying about the East Coast side; you have good men there, trust them. Like I've said many times, the West Coast war is primarily a distraction, intended to keep us from paying attention to the real threat, but it's a critical front all the same – if we lose San Francisco or Los Angeles, we're pretty much done for. I'm charging you with eliminating the Pacific threat." Adrian paused for a moment. "I'd give you a promotion to go with it, but you're already in charge of all of our military forces... but if you want my job?" he said with a shrug.

"Hell no! I don't want your job, and you can't make me take it." The Admiral replied with a smile.

"No harm in trying... might've caught you in an insane moment." Adrian returned the smile somewhat grimly.

A knock on the Admiral's door and an ensign came in with a sheet of paper. "Message for you sir!" he said, handing the paper to the Admiral before leaving the room.

The Admiral read from the document, a frown slowly growing on his face. "Full Naval battle off Hawaii. Chinese warships trying to take the islands. We've responded with our warships and are giving them a fast and brutal lesson." The Admiral paused for a moment and looked at Adrian. "Now why would they do that? Surely they knew it was a suicide mission?"

Adrian sat back in his chair and thought for a moment. "Maybe their intelligence isn't as good as we thought. Maybe they thought our warships were out hitting tankers like they had originally intended. It's either that or a feint of some kind. What could they be up to that they wanted to draw us into a battle there?" Adrian shook his head. "I don't like it. Beef up the coastal watch – both coasts – make sure there isn't any place that's not covered. They may be hoping to draw warships out from the Pacific coast to Hawaii, so they can try to get inside of them."

The Admiral picked up his phone and issued the orders. Hanging it back up he asked, "Could it be possible that their intelligence is that bad?"

"I don't know. Surely they've received radio reports of the explosive boat tactic. They must know what we're doing. Hell, we *know* they do. That's why they spread out their tankers so much. But they might think our Navy is more fragile than it is, or that we have fewer warships than we actually have. I hope that's true anyway. Certainly it's an expensive diversion, if diversion was their goal. If that's the case, then they're up to something big. It may be time to put a few aircraft up and scout the zone between shore and where we've found ships. Take the submarines we've held in reserve and put them out there patrolling also. I'm going to rack out, I'm exhausted. Have someone wake me in four hours."

As Adrian stood to leave he remarked, "Looks like I won't see Linda after all. Put that communication group together for me, I'll be flying out in the morning." On his way to his cabin, Adrian stopped at the radio room to put a call through for Linda to be patched in to his cabin. He wasn't looking forward to telling her he wouldn't be home after all.

Two days later Adrian landed at Point Mugu Naval Air Station, just north of Los Angeles. The Base Commander greeted Adrian on the air strip.

"Welcome to Point Mugu sir! I've got ground transport right here, we can go straight to HQ." Adrian returned the Captain's salute then shook his hand. "Thank you Captain. Let's roll."

As they settled in at the conference table Adrian unrolled a large map of the Pacific Ocean. "Captain..."

"Please sir, just Tim."

"I'm here, Tim, because the naval battle off Hawaii makes no sense, makes me suspicious. I'm thinking it has to be a diversionary tactic. My best guess is that they're trying to divert us from either San Francisco or Los Angeles. Those two cities have the largest concentration of refineries on the West coast. Oil is the immediate target, and they're not going to ship back unrefined petroleum when they can gin up a few refineries and ship back refined fuels instead. The ports at Los Angeles will be easier for a fleet of tankers to get to than the ports at San Francisco. Somewhat easier, neither presents any particular problems for them. But I think Los Angeles will be target number one. I'll camp out here a few days with you and see what happens, ride along on a few of your aerial scouting missions. Then I'm heading for the east coast."

Adrian looked down from the cockpit at the ships far below. The plane had reached the halfway point of its fuel reserve just after they spotted the Chinese fleet of tankers and merchant vessels. Adrian estimated two-hundred ships, a lot closer to the coast than anyone had imagined. As the plane turned back to base the pilot radioed in the coordinates. Radar gave them the fleet's speed. Back at Mugu they would plot intercept courses for fast boat deployment up and down the coast. Within forty-eight hours the Chinese ships would be under attack.

A Jeep rolled up as the jet taxied to a stop at Mugu on a nearly empty fuel tank and Adrian climbed out of the cockpit. "The Admiral needs you on the radio sir," shouted the driver.

Minutes later Adrian was in the operations room talking to the Admiral. "Adrian, we've spotted three fleets similar to the one you just spotted, but off the east coast. They're coming in, fast and in large numbers."

"Where are they headed?" Adrian asked.

"They're more or less headed for third points along the coast. Can't say specifically where – could be planning to land at remote locations and establish beach-heads. Too soon to tell."

"Have we spotted anything moving towards the Gulf yet? I still think that will be their main target."

"Nothing yet, but they have a lot of islands to hide behind, so I'm not confident that they aren't close in and waiting until we're distracted further north."

"We'll have a surprise waiting for them when they make that move. I'll be in Charleston as soon as I can get there."

Within two hours Adrian was back in the F16-D heading east, stopping briefly in Oklahoma for refueling before getting back in the air. Adrian had just fallen asleep when he was awakened by a strident alarm blaring in his ears. Opening his eyes he saw the pilot quickly hitting switches. "Adrian!" the pilot shouted into his microphone. "We're going to eject in four seconds. Remember the drill and *hold on!*"

Adrian barely had time to comprehend the meaning of the words "We're going to eject" when he was blasted by an explosion that ripped off the canopy above his head and then he was struck by a tremendous force from below. Once out of the plane, a drogue gun in the seat would fire a metal slug that pulled a small parachute, called a drogue parachute, out of the top of the chair. This would slow Adrian's rate of descent and stabilize the seat's altitude and trajectory. After a very short amount of time, the altitude sensor would cause the drogue parachute to pull the main parachute from Adrian's chute pack. At this point, a seat-man-separator motor would fire and the seat would fall away from him. This sequence of actions would only take a few seconds, some of them separated by only micro-seconds.

Faster than his mind could comprehend, Adrian was shooting up and out of the cockpit into a massive wind force that felt like it was ripping his clothes and skin from him. Still sitting in the "chair," he had a rocket strapped to his butt that was accelerating him up and out of the cockpit, away from the F-16, creating horrific g-forces. His body was embroiled in too many sensations coming at him too fast for his mind to follow.

Then suddenly he was separated from the seat, hanging from a parachute. The upward momentum had ceased and he now began drifting rapidly down to earth. Silence fell like a blow. He watched the F-16 spiral into the ground a thousand yards in front of him. It crashed with horrendous impact; ripping the fragile metal into thousands of pieces blown in all directions as a huge fire-ball erupted, followed by a column of thick black smoke. And then he hit the ground himself with an impact that jarred every molecule in his body.

Adrian was shaken. Only a few short seconds before he had been sound asleep; his mind was still catching up to the reality of what happened. His body was further behind on catching up than his mind. Disoriented both mentally and physically from the wild experience, he unlatched the parachute harness and pulled off the helmet and face mask, then forced himself to crawl a few feet, and vomited. Emptying his stomach Adrian rolled over onto his back and took a slow assessment of his body. He wiggled his toes then worked his way up to his neck. Finding everything working he also found he was sore over every inch of his body.

Then he remembered the pilot. Adrian quickly sat up. Brushing off a wave of dizziness, he shoved himself to a wobbly stand and looked around. He spotted the other parachute draped across a tree several hundred yards away and moved as fast as he could towards it. As he got closer, he could see the pilot lying on the ground, not moving. A foreboding struck Adrian. He began running and arrived breathing hard and dizzy.

Harold was unconscious, possibly dead. Adrian carefully felt for a pulse in his wrist; he didn't dare move the pilot's head to get to his carotid artery, he was afraid he might make a spinal injury worse, if there was one. He found the pulse, strong enough that Adrian let out a long breath he hadn't realized he was holding. Harold wasn't dead. But his left leg was broken, the shin bent at a sickening angle. While Adrian sorely wanted to remove his friend from the straps holding him in, he knew the better approach was to wait and see if consciousness returned on its own, and then perform a full assessment for other injuries with his help. Concerned that the wind might gust and catch in the parachute then drag the pilot across the rough ground Adrian cut the parachute cords from the harness.

While waiting for Harold to regain consciousness, Adrian decided to reset the leg bone, hoping to avoid the pain he would surely go through if awake. Adrian found two straight tree limbs and cut them down with his bowie knife, choosing green wood that would bend a little and give some shock protection. With the sticks cut he then cut parachute cord to tie the make-shift splint in place.

As gently as he could, he pulled outwards on the ankle with one hand, using the other hand to feel the broken bone. The pilot thrashed around without wakening. Each time Adrian pulled, the Harold thrashed, often groaning. Bit by bit Adrian returned the bone to its proper place, as nearly as he could tell. Adrian watched him closely for several minutes afterwards. He still hadn't awakened and Adrian was now worried about concussion and shock. Gently lifting each eyelid he checked the pupils, they were both the same size, possibly indicating a mild instead of severe concussion.

Adrian took an inventory of what they had to work with survival-wise. He and the pilot each had a pistol, the bowie knife strapped to Adrian's hip that he was never without, good clothing and sturdy boots. He had more than enough for an extended hike. He re-created as much as he could of their last position. From the terrain he'd seen during his descent and the track they'd been on, it looked to him like they were in the Ouachita Mountains, a remote National Forest in Arkansas. Chances of finding motorized transportation would be zilch.

Walking would be the only way out, and with the war heating up Adrian was already in a hurry to get.moving.

He sat down and waited patiently for the pilot to awaken. He couldn't think of any way to speed that process up that might not cause more damage. He didn't want to be gone when the pilot awakened; he wanted to be there to reassure him and to see what other injuries he may have suffered. The pilot was breathing and his heart was pumping and there were no other visible injuries to work on so it was a matter of waiting. Adrian built a small fire, and retrieved the parachute fabric to have something to do while he waited.

Thirty minutes later, the pilot's hands began to twitch, then a loud groan and his eyes fluttered open. Obviously disoriented he stared at Adrian for a moment, blinking his eyes. He was young and fit and came about rapidly. He removed his face mask and said "What?"

Adrian was so relieved he laughed at him. "What? We ejected and the plane crashed. You've been out for a while. Your leg is broken. Other than that Mrs. Lincoln, how did you like the play?"

The pilot looked at him in confusion.

"How do you feel?" Adrian asked.

"Woozy, but pretty much okay." He began to remove the straps.

Adrian said, "Hold up, don't move yet, let's get an inventory first." Adrian talked him through slight movements of all of his body parts, focusing especially on his neck. Everything checked out so Adrian removed the straps and helped him stand up, steadying him with an arm around his chest.

"Damn the luck," Harold said quietly. Looking at Adrian he said, "Engine failed. Don't know why. Didn't have any luck re-starting it and we were going down like a rock. Don't recall anything after that."

"You woke me up and said we were ejecting, next thing I know we were shooting through the air while the plane fell away below us. It hit hard, total loss. I think we're in Arkansas, that sound right to you?"

"Yeah, we were about over the middle of the mountain range when all hell broke loose. Sorry, I meant to say 'sir'... still a little rattled."

"Call me 'sir' again and you'll have a hell of a fight on your hands. Call me Adrian. We've got work to do and we're going to have to do it the hard way, and together. No formalities are going to make this go any better."

"Gotcha. Well you're the survival expert sir, what do you suggest?"

Adrian replied, "I suggest we get the hell back to the war as fast as we can. You're not going to be able to walk, though, so I'll rig up a travois from the parachutes and a couple of poles. I'll drag you out. We move as long as there's enough light to see. We've got to get back fast. Was there time for you to send out a radio message?"

"No, no time at all. They won't know something is wrong until we don't show up, which should have been about now, but they won't have a clue what happened or where. They'll look for us, but it's not likely they'll find us. We don't file flight plans anymore, so they'll only know the general line of flight. Chances of them spotting the wreckage are somewhere between none and no way. There'll be survival packs that dropped from the ejection seats somewhere around here. In them is a beacon that we can carry with us, but since it was designed to work off satellite transmission, I doubt it'll do us any good. The survival packs also have a compass, and I always keep maps in mine. We can navigate to wherever we want to go, once we get a fix on our location."

Adrian replied, "We won't need to have too specific of a fix, we'll head east, and at some point we'll come across a road or highway; then we can get that solid fix from the road signs. Come on, let's find those survival packs and get moving."

Looking down at his splinted leg, the pilot said, "You need to get back as soon as humanly possible, but I don't; I'm out of action for months." He grimaced as pain shot up his broken leg. Gasping for breath he tried to sit down, Adrian helped him. "Look" Harold said "I'll slow you down to a crawl, and being dragged around doesn't sound like a pleasant experience. You need to go on. You can send help back to me. The faster you get out the faster you can send help back. Help might arrive sooner that way than you can get me out."

Adrian replied, "Yeah, already thought of that. Problem is that you're going to be in too much pain to take care of yourself – and if an infection sets in, you'll be delirious with fever. We don't have much in the way of survival rations and you won't be able to get your own food. We don't know how long it'll take me to walk out of here, could be a long time. With no one to look after you... you could easily be dead before anyone can get back here. Not to mention there may be wolves or bears to contend with, and you wouldn't be able to fight them off. I've tried to think of another way and I can't. I'll take you with me."

"No sir. You're needed back immediately. I refuse to slow you down. I'm staying here. I'll be fine." The pilot grimaced and moaned as another wave of pain hit him. After it passed he continued, "And even if I die it's small potatoes compared to the war... the number of our men that might be killed while you drag me out... I don't want that on my conscience. Lord knows what's happening out there and you need to get back in control of the situation. Just drag me to a water source, leave half the rations, then hurry out."

"You'd make a fine lawyer." Adrian said with a smile meant to ease the sting of his next words. "But you don't have a choice in the matter. There's no way I can leave you here like this. No way."

Adrian began making the travois. He cut down two long skinny poles and using part of the parachute and parachute cord he attached the rig to his parachute harness. Strapping the harness on he could pull the travois while keeping his arms free. It was crude, but it was effective transportation for the wounded pilot.

CHAPTER 15

SIX DAYS OF DRAGGING HAROLD on the travois across rough, mountainous terrain left them both exhausted and hungry. It was hard slogging, and in places impassible for the travois, many places too steep or the brush too thick. Adrian had to divert course several times each day. The survival rations were long gone, but they had found water frequently as they traveled, and, in fact had to cross several streams. Adrian carried the pilot on his back across the creeks, then waded back for the travois. They had to swim one river as they headed south towards Highway 270, which the pilot's maps showed would eventually take them to Hot Springs. Adrian swam the river with the pilot on his back, an arduous task. Then back across the river to get the travois, then across the river again carrying the bundled travois. Once they came out of the mountain range the land leveled by comparison and they made better progress.

Each evening Adrian set up camp near water and would fish, using the emergency fishing kits from the survival packs. He caught few fish; he had better luck setting snares, catching four rabbits and a raccoon along the way. Adrian foraged at each stop, adding edible plants to the stewed meats.

Amaranth, cattail roots, purslane, and sorrel were generally abundant if you knew what they were and where to look. Adrian knew. Mixed in with fish or critter meat, the plants added needed vitamins, phytochemicals and nutrients. They were not tasty dishes, but they were healthy and available.

Harold had descended into feverish incoherence. Adrian stopped when the pilot's fever seemed to be skyrocketing. He set the pilot up as comfortably as possible and went herb hunting. He soon found an area with feverwort growing in abundance. Gathering several pounds of the fever-reducing plant, he continued looking until along a nearby creek he found willow trees whose bark he could use for both pain relief and additional fever reducing properties. Returning to camp he made a bowl of willow bark and boiled the feverwort inside it, keeping the bark bowl filled with water to keep it from burning. The resulting elixir served as a dual purpose pain and fever reducer. Adrian tasted it – it was bitter and unpleasant – then cajoled the pilot into drinking it. The results were not dramatic, but there was a definite easing of the pain and lowering of the fever. Adrian packed the bark and leaves to carry with them and made a new cooking pot each evening from the willow bark so that each new batch of the elixir had a fresh infusion of the plant's medicinal properties. Adrian stopped several times each day to give the pilot more of the infusion, followed by copious amounts of fresh water.

When they finally reached the highway Adrian was jubilant. He turned east and began a routine of double timing for fifteen minutes followed by fast walking for fifteen minutes. The smooth asphalt surface was far easier on the pilot but the wooden poles began to wear away quickly and had to be periodically replaced. After a day and a half of this they were both beyond exhausted, but Adrian kept pushing. He had a war to get to.

During the afternoon of the second day on the highway Adrian saw three trucks approaching in the distance. Pistols wouldn't be enough against rifles or a large band of men, but Adrian was determined to get back into action and decided to wave them down – even though they were going in the opposite direction. As the vehicles got closer, they became recognizable as military trucks.

The trucks ground to a halt and the first driver jumped out and ran up to Adrian. "Shit!" He said, then "Sorry, Mr. President, but I am just so damn happy to see you."

Adrian responded with a broad smile. "'Shit' is appropriate son. The pilot needs immediate attention. He's running a high fever. What in the hell are you doing out here though?"

"Looking for you, sir. Air searches didn't turn up anything, so some brass-head decided that we should drive up and down this highway. Given where they thought you might have been when you crashed, they thought you might have survived and would probably walk out this way. We've been driving up and down a four-hundred mile stretch for a week now." The soldier stopped talking and scratched his chin. With a broad grin he continued, "And damned if the brass-heads weren't right for a change. We have a medical team with us, they'll take care of the pilot. What else can we do for you other than getting you back to base?"

"Food and a radio"

"Yes sir. Let me call in – there's a chopper waiting." The soldier turned to the man next to him and said, "Shorty, get the medics out of the truck. Rustle up some grub, get the best of the MREs."

An hour later Adrian and the pilot were strapped into the back of the helicopter. The F-16 pilot fell asleep as the helicopter carried them to Hot Springs. Adrian put on the radio headset for his seat and asked the chopper pilot to get him in contact with the Admiral.

"Adrian!" The Admiral said with relief. "I'm damn glad you're back in the saddle. Are you okay? Any injuries?"

"I'm fine Admiral. The pilot has a broken leg and is feverish, but he's getting full medical attention now. What's the war news?"

"It's not good. We've got two major actions going on the West Coast. One near Los Angeles and one near San Francisco. We're not quite holding our own. They've come up with a defense that's playing hell with the attack boats. They've mounted chain guns on mobile platforms on the decks. They can wheel the chain guns into any position rapidly. They're blowing most of our boats up before they can hit the ships."

"Have you come up with a counter?"

"We hit them with multiple boats on all sides as we talked about in Hawaii. That way some of them still get through, but they're chewing our boats up faster than we can make new ones and they're moving damn close. We've called in as many militias as we can, getting them ready for a ground war at the ports. Most of our special operations-trained soldiers have been deployed as advisers among the militias. We're vulnerable between the ports. We're maintaining coastal spotters and will be able to react to only some of those invasion points, but it will be a slower and smaller reaction since several of the fighting forces are at the two primary ports."

"How long before they reach the ports, Admiral?"

"Two days at the current pace. Are you still sure you want to reserve the Naval forces?"

"Where are their naval assets right now?"

"They're still out at sea. Apparently they won't move them in until they have to. They could be here in three days if they want to."

"Then reserve your ships for when they come in, if they do. I'm not at all certain they will. But if they do, you'll want everything you have to welcome them with. And the East Coast?"

"Bloody hell there Adrian. Instead of clustering into definite locations they've spread out and are coming at the coast in a dozen or more locations, and none of them make immediate strategic sense. They're close in, maybe three days out at most from making landfall."

"They're obviously planning a series of land invasions," Adrian said. "Off-loading ground troops that will sync up somewhere into a massive occupation army. What about the Gulf? Any movement there?"

"Yes, and I wanted to save that for last. They're coming in on both sides of Cuba by the hundreds. You were right that they would try to distract us and then come in there with their heaviest assault. The only good news is that you still have a little bit of time to get back to Texas where the main action is going to be. We have a three front war going on. West Coast, East Coast and the Gulf of Mexico. I'm overseeing the West Coast, Admiral Rutherford is over the East Coast and now that you're back you have the Gulf. You have the worst of it coming at you. It's grit time, Adrian. Nothing but fighting to do now."

"Got it Admiral. Soon as we land, I'll get transport home. We'll stay in radio contact throughout. I need to call Linda now and let her know I'm okay."

The trainer jet carried Adrian from Hot Springs to Corpus Christi in short order. Adrian took a Jeep from the landing strip to the dock where he hopped onto a swift boat that carried him to the carrier. It had the best overall communication system available, and Adrian needed that capability.

Adrian entered the war room and looked at the maps. Two massive Chinese fleets were marked on it. They were indeed coming from both sides of Cuba and would be in the Gulf in no more than a day and a half.

Adrian turned to the ship's new Captain, a fortyish man with steely eyes and a crisp manner. He had been sent in by the Admiral just a week before. "Captain Morgan?" Adrian asked with no hint of a smile.

"Yes Mr. President. Believe me I've heard them all sir, although I wouldn't mind hearing a new one sir."

"I wouldn't dream of trying." Adrian said, now with a small smile. "Give me a full briefing."

"Yes sir. We have attack boat fleets ready and raring to go. They're scattered up and down the Gulf Coast, a dozen on the Mexican side. As the Chinese enter the Gulf we'll begin deploying them in stages. From the reports we've gotten on the number of attack boat losses in other places it appears we do not have enough to entirely stop them. I'd say we can knock out seventy-five percent of the Chinese before we run out, but that leaves a lot to deal with. We've staged militias at strategic points that can react rapidly to landings. Their troops will outnumber ours significantly when they make landfall. It's not looking real good sir. That is unless we can use our naval assets, then we have a better chance."

"We may get to that point Morgan, but I want them held in reserve for the day the Chinese send in their Navy. It's still a matter of not depleting our ammunition too soon."

"As you say, sir."

"Captain, I'm going to my quarters for a few hours of rest. Would you get me in radio contact with my wife?"

"Absolutely sir, no problem."

"That's great baby, glad to hear everything is quiet at home. How's the experiment going with the Chinese soldier?"

"It's an odd thing. The entire village is in on the act and so far there haven't been any obvious mistakes. For all intents and purposes, he thinks he is in a post-war village and has free run of the place, yet most people pretty much ignore him, just as they would if this was real. His English is good, he communicates well. The kids that "adopted" him are marvelous actors. He hasn't let loose with what his mission was... so to speak, but he's acting as if he believes what he sees."

"I hope he spills the beans soon. Whatever they were up to out there has to have significance. How are the Rangers? Is Race holding up?"

"Oh Adrian, she's a trooper. She took over as second-in-command of the Rangers like a natural and is doing a damn good job. I take care of the day-to-day details, but she's running the operations and doing great. They still go out and stop the bad guys on a routine basis. If anything, this war seems to have brought out more raiders than ever before. There's a lot of food and munitions being transported around, and raiders see that as opportunity. There have been several small convoys hit and some the raiders were strong enough to take. The Rangers are patrolling the convoy routes heavily now, and getting into action almost every day. Having most of the able-bodied fighters in the militias along the coast line gives the bandits a lot more latitude. If it wasn't for the Rangers, they'd have free play."

"Love you babe. I'll sign off and get a few hours' sleep. Talk to you tomorrow."

After a few more moments of intimate talk Adrian turned off the radio, stripped off his travel-stained clothes and took a shower. Two minutes after toweling off he was sound asleep, hoping to get a few hours' sleep before bad news knocked at his cabin door.

CHAPTER 16

ADRIAN AWOKE IMMEDIATELY FROM A deep dream at the first of the three rapid knocks to the bulkhead door. As he pulled on a pair of clean undershorts, he said "Come in."

Captain Morgan entered quickly. "Sorry to awaken you, sir, but we have new reports that you need to hear."

"Tell me." Adrian said.

"We have reports of a land-based Chinese army, a large one, moving across the border from Mexico near Del Rio sir. Best estimates – and they are from rough sources – is five hundred men, fully mechanized. Moving north rapidly."

"Do we have air assets to hit them with or at least to get better intel?"

"Nothing to hit them with sir, only a couple of spotters already on the way out there; they should be reporting back within minutes."

"Let's get up to the tactical room." Adrian finished dressing and followed the Captain out.

Adrian listened to the radio report as the pilot flew high over the enemy convoy. "I see about a hundred trucks, dozens of fuel tankers, heavy trucks carrying artillery. Looks like ten trucks with medium range missiles. They're moving at fifty-miles-per-hour. They're on Highway 90 moving northwest. They'll reach the junction of Highway 163 in half an hour. Can't hang around any longer, running close on fuel."

"You get pictures?" Adrian asked.

"Yes sir, a lot of them."

"Transmit the photos and hurry back, we may need you to fuel up and go out again. Good job, and thank you."

"Yes sir, banking east now. Be back in forty-five minutes."

Adrian turned to Morgan. "This has to tie in with our Chinese prisoner back at Fort Brazos. Get me a radio link to them."

Two minutes later Adrian was talking to the intelligence officer in charge of the Chinese prisoner. "Lieutenant, we've just gotten a look at a large Chinese military contingent moving across the border into southern Texas, near Del Rio. This has to tie in with the scouting mission your prisoner was on. I need to know the goal of his mission. I still can't understand it having anything to do with Lubbock; there's nothing there that would help them. I have a bad feeling about where they are actually heading, and I need confirmation right now. If they're going where I think they're going... we're going to have a hell of a time intercepting them with enough strength to do us any good. I don't want to mobilize in the wrong place. Get that information in the next four hours, any way you can, but get it."

"Yes sir. I'll have it for you, if it's at all possible."

"Hurry it up, time is beyond critical."

Adrian handed the microphone back to the radio man. Turning to the Captain, Adrian said, "Morgan, we're going to have to mobilize and move at least a thousand men in the next few hours, two thousand would be better, but I need at least a thousand in place to intercept and hold the Chinese while we bring in more." Pointing to a spot on the map, Adrian said, "I want two hundred right here, send the others here." Adrian pointed to a second place on the map. "We have to get our men in place ahead of them. Start mobilizing."

"Yes sir, but may I point out that it will seriously weaken our shoreline defenses, and apparently for not much. What possible strategic gain is there for the Chinese to take a semi-desert area with a low population density?"

"Get the troops moving, I'll explain when I hear back from Fort Brazos."

Three anxious hours later Adrian was again talking to the Lieutenant at Fort Brazos, "I sat the prisoner down with me and had lunch. I figured I would just ask him casually and if that didn't work we'd go to more extreme measures. Turns out he was willing to talk – this "war's over" ruse worked. He didn't have a clue what we've done to him. As a result, I believe we can rely on this information as solid. He said that they were scouting a route to Amarillo. He doesn't know what was interesting about Amarillo to the higher-ups, no one on his mission knew. Just that Amarillo was the ultimate goal."

"Thank you Lieutenant. Your team performed excellently. It confirms what I feared. Give your men a well-earned pat on the back for me."

"Yes sir, will do, and thank you. If I may ask,

what's important about Amarillo? And what do we do with the prisoner, sir?"

"I'd rather not say over the radio, you'll get a full brief when you get here. Bring the prisoner with you, put him in the brig. Get here as soon as you can."

Adrian paused for a long moment after handing off the microphone. "Morgan, how much progress in mobilizing troops?"

"ETA is four days sir."

"Make it two. Make that happen, or there's not much point in going. This has to be a full-out effort, use every resource available. This takes priority over the invasion fleet defense."

"Yes sir, it will happen as you say. May I ask what's so important about Amarillo?"

"There's nothing strategically important to the Chinese about Amarillo, Morgan. But close by is Pantex. And *Pantex* is very strategically important to the Chinese – and to us."

"Sir, I've heard the name, but I don't know what it is."

"I'll explain over dinner. I'm starving."

"Pantex, Captain." Adrian said after eating half his fried fish, "Is a nuclear weapons assembly and disassembly facility. The only one of its kind. The bottom line is there are over twelve-thousand nuclear pits currently in storage there. Twelve thousand nuclear war heads that the Chinese can activate... and use. Imagine the devastation they can cause with those if China gets control of Pantex." Adrian paused and then said softly, "We are finished. They will be able to fire nuclear-tipped missiles that can reach anywhere on the content from there. The invasion fleet has been one large diversion. They can lose every ship, every man, and even their own Navy, and still win hands down if they get that facility. Once they have it, they'll ship most of the devices back to China to use against the Russians. This would give them the edge there."

"Jesus, sir."

"Jesus, indeed. As soon as you have the first troops moving, you will get another thousand men and every bit of fighting equipment you can find to Pantex to secure it. I doubt that the troop movement we spotted is going to be the only one. Hell, they can send troops from the Gulf of California or anywhere in Mexico to meet up with the one we spotted. And they surely will. They won't rely on just one force, they'll have at least two and probably three forces moving in, meeting up near Pantex to secure it. They'll have other forces in Mexico staged to move in with missiles and possibly bomber aircraft. They'll be bringing technicians and scientists to assemble the explosive triggers for the pits. Every damn thing they need is collected behind defenses that are paper thin. Chain link fences aren't going to slow them down. They'll be happy to take a ninety-percent casualty rate, but unless we get there right now and prepare for them they won't lose two-percent."

"Why meet them at Lamesa, sir?" Morgan asked, pointing to the spot on the map Adrian had identified for the troops to gather.

"If you look at the road map," replied Adrian, "and they have to stick to roads, all roads from

where they are to Pantex pretty much go through Lamesa. They'd have to swing way wide to go around it. But even if they do, from Lamesa we can swing with them. Lamesa is going to be a rough fight. These won't be regular soldiers, these are going to be well trained, well-armed, and dedicated troops. These will be their best men, reserved especially for this mission. They'll have teams out in front of them, clearing the way, securing bridges and the small towns they go through. This battle, the battle for Pantex is what this war is really about; they'll spare nothing to get it. The invasion fleets still have to be dealt with, but this is priority number one, and there is no close second priority. We can lose every oil well and refinery if we have to. We'll get them back later... if there is a later. But we cannot lose Pantex."

Adrian looked down at the table. He knew this would be his last decent meal for a long time. "Morgan, the Gulf is your war to fight now. I'm going to Lamesa. Alert the communications team to go with me. We need immediate focus on where the other invasion army is coming from. As soon as it's spotted, we'll need troops on the ground in front of them, so assemble them now and put them on red alert to move out instantly. Our strategy is fairly simple: Intercept them before they get to Pantex, and destroy them or slow them down while we're building up a defense at Pantex itself. Is that clear?"

Morgan looked Adrian dead in the eye. "Crystal clear sir. Count on me to make it happen."

Adrian looked long and hard into Morgan's eyes. "I am. And there's one more thing I need you to make happen." Adrian then explained in detail what he needed.

Adrian drove down Highway 137 from Stanton to Lamesa. "This land is so flat you can see tomorrow to the East and Yesterday to the West." Adrian said to Race.

On his way to Lamesa Adrian had stopped at Fort Brazos. He had spent a precious hour with Linda, after telling Race to pick her two best Rangers to go with him to act as scouts.

Adrian turned the truck around and started back to Lamesa. They were silent until Adrian pulled off the road in the South side of town. He stopped next to a small dry wash that crossed the road. Getting out of the truck he looked around. All he saw was flat land covered with sporadic mesquite trees and the occasional residence or storage shed. "This is the best cover I've seen and it's no cover at all. We would be better off going back further into town if there weren't so many side streets they could use to avoid us. At least here we can see them maneuver. But they can see us too. Poor as it is, it's our only option."

Race replied. "It's damn poor. Everyone will be exposed. This little draw will only afford minimal protection. Once we move out of it we're wide open on all sides."

"I know. We're going to hit them here and pull back immediately, then hit them again and again as opportunity and terrain permit. We won't get in a decisive battle here, but we can cripple them a bit if we play it right."

"I don't see any way to play it at all Adrian. It's just a flat spot with no cover. If you see a plan here what is it?"

"Oh, I see a plan, and a decent one at that. I need to know how long that convoy is. How spread out are they? When they come to a halt how far apart do they spread out? Get on the radio and check in with Corpus Christi, see if they've had any opportunities to figure that out. If not we'll do the best we can with the aerial photos."

A few minutes later Race reported, "They don't have much better information than the photos. So far they've only been spotted traveling. What do you have in mind?"

Adrian explained his attack plan.

CHAPTER 17

ADRIAN WATCHED AS THE CHINESE convoy came into sight a mile down the road. "Race, remind each operator to mind their own marks and wait until the first explosion, the one closest to us. Then they are to fire at will, as soon as they can."

Race sent out a short radio message to the waiting men and women. They were scattered out along a line more-or-less perpendicular to the road. Each had taken a vantage point that allowed them to see a particular spot on the road. "Done Adrian, what next?"

"Nothing next. We wait and follow the plan."

"Two minutes to target zone, Adrian," Race reported. "They're moving slower, probably because they're coming into a town. I really don't like letting their forward patrol past us, don't like having them behind us."

"All part of the plan. We know where they are, and when they come back, after we attack the convoy, we'll be ready for them. Ready as we can be."

The two minutes went by quickly. As the first truck in the convoy reached a point fifty-yards before the draw, Adrian depressed a signal generator. *Boom!* The first truck was blown upwards two feet and crashed back down a smoking ruin. Fire tore through the truck as the fuel tank burst and exploded into flames. Almost instantly after the first IED exploded, a series of explosions ripped through the convoy most of the way back. The IED's had been placed under the center of the road, spread out at a distance designed to imitate the normal spacing of the convoy. The asphalt patches where the IED's had been dug in were works of camouflage art, barely discernible even if you knew where to look. Using spray paint found in an abandoned hardware store, and dirt, they were nearly invisible. In less than three seconds, twenty furious eruptions followed Adrian's blast.

Then the guerrilla teams on each side of the road opened up, sending bullets screaming into the trucks. Following Adrian's orders to eliminate as much of the enemy's artillery as possible, shoulder-launched rockets fired into the artillery trucks in a series of bruising explosions that ripped through much of the Chinese's equipment, putting a few of them out of commission.

Snipers fired fifty-caliber armor piercing rounds into truck engines, attempting to disable them on the spot. Even so, the Chinese seriously outnumbered the Texas Militia, and on Adrian's orders, the militia immediately pulled back and moved north as soon as return fire began to pick up. Adrian stood to lose too many soldiers in a sustained fire-fight. His strategy was to hit and withdraw, move to the next location and hit again, guerrilla-style. His plan was to do this over and over all the way back to Pantex if he had to. The Chinese convoy was damaged, but far from out.

The Chinese would now face the choice of either slowing down significantly, or moving along as fast as they could. Either option played well for the defenders. Slowing them down bought time that was desperately needed. If they didn't slow down they were easier to hit.

Another force of a dozen soldiers were ready for the Chinese forward patrol that had passed by earlier. As the militia rapidly moved north leaving the smoking convoy behind they also moved into pre-planned positions waiting for the forward patrol to be contacted by their convoy and return. The patrol was back in less than ten minutes, moving at a high rate of speed.

As they entered the north side of town, they were hit from all sides by heavy small-arms fire and a half-dozen rocket launchers. They were wiped out within seconds. But the convoy was coming up rapidly, so Adrian had every soldier load into pre-positioned vehicles and speed away to the north again. Only a few spotters remained behind, hidden at the major road junctions. If the convoy didn't take Highway 87 towards Lubbock, the most direct route towards Pantex, then Adrian would know as soon as they took a different road. There weren't many alternate routes.

Race's Rangers had previously scouted the next ambush spot along the road the Chinese would probably take. Soldiers were already nearly finished installing IEDs there. Other locations further north were being scouted, and the IED teams would move on to the north as soon as they could. The Chinese would know what to expect, but not exactly where.

Forward patrols would be attacked wherever they were found; there were enough soldiers and firepower to eliminate the enemy patrols, and the Chinese commander would soon learn it was useless to send them out.

While scrambling to get to the next attack point Adrian received a radio call from Corpus Christi. "Mr. President, we've spotted another invasion force as you forecasted. It must have come from the Gulf of California. At the moment it is approaching Santa Rosa, New Mexico, traveling east on Interstate 40."

"What size is the convoy?" Adrian asked grimly.

"A bit larger than the one you're already dealing with sir."

"Have you deployed our second group yet?"

"They're in the air now. Where do you want them to land?"

"I'll get a map and call you back."

Ten minutes later Adrian called Corpus Christi. "Captain, land them east of Tucumcari, at Plaza Larga Creek. There's a bit of terrain there, and overpasses we can blow as they cross. Tell them to rig the bridges as soon as they land. I have transport; I'll be there a little after they are. Contact the Admiral to expect a call from me when I'm in the air."

Adrian turned to Race, "Get half your troops on the plane and brief the other half on how to continue here."

Race nodded, and then said "Suppose you get killed. What happens to the rest of us? You're the glue holding this whole war together, Adrian, risking your life is crazy. When your plane went down in the mountains and we didn't hear from you...

we thought you were dead. The wind went out of everyone's sails."

"If I'd been killed, someone else would have stepped up and carried on, Race," Adrian replied. "It's always that way, always will be. But sitting in front of a big war board and moving troops around like chess pieces is not going to work, at least not for me. My job, as I see it, is to be at the front edge of developing threats, coming up with strategies and tactics as those threats evolve. Just like here. Now that our resistance pattern has developed and the troops know what to do, it's time to move on and do it all over again. Everyone here understands their missions now, how to tactically engage the enemy. Think of it like coaching, because that's essentially what I am doing. Once I get the team to a certain point, I move on to the next team, the next threat.

"The Admiral has the West Coast, Rutherford has the East Coast and Morgan has the Gulf. All good men, all extremely capable. They know what to do. We have Pantex, and it's the most critical of all of our missions. We lose Pantex we lose the war, Race... and I don't intend to lose Pantex.

Adrian talked to the Admiral throughout the entire short flight. The Admiral gave him a briefing on the state of the war on both coasts; it wasn't good news. Chinese ships were slipping through and landing large fighting forces. At least five had made landfall so far, two on the West Coast and three on the East Coast. Troops were being diverted to intercept and fight, but none had arrived yet. The Admiral sounded like he was trying not to sound downcast about it. The Admiral didn't understand land warfare nearly as well as naval warfare.

Adrian told him to hang tough, keep his ships ready, and to let the militias take care of the land war. "It looks to be a long, hard war, Admiral, and it's going to look a lot worse before it gets better. But the Chinese ground troops have a couple of major problems. They have no resupply lines, and they can only hold the ground they stand on. We'll bring them down by attrition, I guarantee it. Just keep their landings to the absolute minimum. We're about to land, I'll call you back later."

Adrian's C-130 landed on Interstate 40, five miles west of Plaza Larga Creek. The Texas border was twenty miles behind their landing spot; Pantex a mere one-hundred-twenty miles away. There weren't many good places to hit the convoy between here and Pantex, so this had to be a hard hit. Adrian had less than one-hundred troops to work with this time – half of the air-lift hadn't been able to get off the ground at Corpus Christi due to an engine malfunction. Operational aircraft were scarce, getting scarcer with every flight; and they were scattered up and down the coasts with no time to get to Corpus Christi and then to this remote New Mexican spot.

Adrian had called Corpus Christi on arrival and told Morgan, "We'll slow them down, but they're already damn close. As soon as I get this operation up and running, I'm heading to Pantex."

The Plaza Larga Creek area where Interstate 40 crosses over was a desolate stretch of seem-desert.

The "creek" was bone dry. There were two short, low bridges on the Interstate crossing the wide, sandy-bottom creek, one for each direction of traffic. A few hundred yards to the south was old Route 66, and it had a small bridge as well. Adrian would blow that bridge, too, not because the convoy would be coming down it, but to keep them from using it after they blew the Interstate bridges. . Concrete panels lined the west side of the creek for a short way either side of the two bridges.

Turning to Race, Adrian pointed at the concrete panels lining the west side of the creek flanking the Interstate bridges. "They won't be stopped here long," he said. "They can move over past those panels and cross without a lot of trouble. Might bog in the sand some, but with the manpower they have they won't stayed bogged-down long. When they get back on the pavement they'll speed up considerably to make up for lost time. That gives us very little time to set the next ambush. We're going to hit them with IEDs while we drop the bridges, then we're out of here. No small arms attack this time, not enough time or personnel."

Adrian directed the IED placements on either side of the bridge in the eastbound lane. While the Chinese had the choice of either lane, they had been staying in the normal lane for their direction of travel. The lanes were widely separated going over the creek. The IEDs were placed before the bridge, taking into account the length of the convoy as it had been relayed to them. There wasn't time to camouflage holes in the road, and the paving here was smooth enough to make that difficult anyway, so they were placed on both shoulders. Instead of the simple explosives they'd used before, here they used fragmentation type IEDs. As Adrian explained to the ordnance group, "Think of them as large claymore mines. The trucks won't be driving directly over them, so the goal is to send shrapnel ripping through the trucks. Shape the charges to get maximum fragmentation spread towards the roadway."

A variety of camouflage techniques were used. Abandoned cars disabled and left from the CME were used where they could be. Clumps of brush in some places, dirt piles in others. The goal was to distribute these in a way that didn't suggest a pattern, it had to look random.

CHAPTER 18

ADRIAN AND RACE HELD THE detonators and waited. Because the IEDs were more of a shotgun approach, they had all been wired to go off together with one button push. But they had to be timed perfectly. Adrian and Race were hidden in the brush on a rise of land a quarter of a mile east of the bridges. They could see the highway for miles. Behind them a mile back, a strike team was ready to ambush the Chinese scout team.

Through dancing heat waves they saw the scout team approaching rapidly. "Here they come." Race said. Adrian was tense.

"Cross your fingers. If the advance team spots the IEDs, this whole plan goes up in smoke and you and I are in for a world of hell." He watched with intense focus as the team approached the IED field, relaxing only slightly as they passed without pausing. "They've had clear sailing all the way to here, they've gotten sloppy. Good."

As the advance team roared by in their open-top vehicles Adrian spotted the convoy in the far distance. "Here comes the main show. Be ready. I'll blow the bridges just before the first truck clears. As soon as I do, you ignite the other IED's."

Within moments, the convoy entered the mine

field. Adrian waited until the lead truck was three-quarters of the way across the bridge, then pushed the detonator. With a huge *crrrump* sound but no visible pyrotechnics the three bridges simultaneously collapsed, taking four trucks into the creek, the last two not yet on the bridge but unable to stop in time. Dust whirled up into the air blocking their view. Then Race hit her detonator and there was a huge explosion of sound, yellow flashes of light showed briefly through the dust, then several columns of black smoke rose above the cloud.

"Let's get moving," Adrian said in a relieved voice.

Throwing the pile of brush from the Jeep they jumped in. Adrian fired it up and raced east on the highway. Ahead they saw more black smoke where the strike team had hit the Chinese forward patrol. As they approached the inferno, they saw Chinese vehicles scattered and burning, hit by IEDs and intense small arms fire. Adrian slowed to wheel between the burning vehicles. Bodies of enemy soldiers were scattered among the vehicles, some on the road and some off to the side. Clearing the debris field Adrian sped up again. The C-130 waited a mile up the road, engines running and loaded with the Texas Ranger and ordnance teams. One militia soldier waited beside the aircraft to take the Jeep on to catch up with the militia at the next ambush point. Adrian and Race jumped into the plane and before they could get settled it was in the air.

Adrian had the pilot circle back and over the Plaza Larga Creek site. Far down below he could see that the convoy was regrouping. A dozen badly damaged vehicles were left where they sat. "If only we had air-power we could wax them easily." Adrian said to Race. "But we're lucky to get anything flying these days."

Adrian had the pilot circle the Pantex plant. "This is just about the flattest place I ever saw," he said to the pilot while standing in the cockpit observing the terrain around the plant. "I don't think there's a rock bigger than a quarter-inch down there, nothing to hide behind for miles, a few shallow draws is all there is for cover."

The pilot asked, "Is that good or bad?"

"Bad... for us," Adrian replied with a grim voice. "It's a level playing field, no pun intended. It means we have to counter their tactics and armor with no cover." The C-130 landed on the paved road next to the Pantex plant.

Adrian was met by a Jeep, and asked the driver to take him to the militia headquarters immediately.

"Lieutenant Frank Matcher, sir!" said the militia's commanding officer, snapping off a smart salute.

"Pleased to meet you, Lieutenant."

Race stepped off the plane at that moment and Frank smiled on seeing her. "Hey Race! Didn't know you'd be here."

Race smiled back. "Didn't know you would either. Think we can talk the Chinese into committing suicide again?"

Adrian looked from Race to Frank, and shook his head. "Give me a disposition report, Lieutenant. We may only have a day, hopefully two, before the fight starts."

Frank was immediately all business. "We arrived yesterday, four hundred militia and my Seal team. We found the permanent security contingent here, and right snappy they are sir, but there are only seventy-five of them. We brought men and small arms and some heavy machine guns. Sir, this place is a disaster to defend. It's wide-open, flat country in all directions. Security is, as you've seen, two tall wire mesh fences – basically nothing. A lot of the complex inside the fence is underground, but a lot is on top and totally exposed. The Chinese can come at us from any and all directions. If they come from all four sides we barely have enough men to mount a defense at all."

"It looks grim Frank, but there are possibilities here. One thing in our favor is that the Chinese are here to capture the facility intact, not destroy it. They will not use artillery on the facility itself, but will use it pinpoint style on the defensive perimeter. What about the scientists and technicians? Are there any left?"

"Yes sir, nearly all of them. Most of them moved their families nearby when they came here to work, and many of the stayed after the CME. There was no good way for them to get home, that's damn rough country out there. There is also quite a stockpile of food, apparently the powers that were saw something of an eventuality and prepared for it. They're growing their own food now – they have deep wells for water and the scientists rigged up a small nuclear power plant that they use to power the entire facility. They have excellent security against normal raiders. No place better for the scientists to be, in all reality.

There's some damn smart people in there. They also seem to have an endless supply of jackrabbits to eat. Not too bad if you're hungry enough, sir."

"Jackrabbits?" Adrian asked.

"Sir, there were jackrabbits inside the fence when it was completed. The fences are electrified. The rabbits did what rabbits do. Sometimes it seems as if you can't walk through there without pushing them out of the way. Real survivors, and imprisoned, so to speak."

"I'll be damned." Adrian said. "Who would've thought of that? Well Frank, as to the scientists – and I've always wanted to say this – take me to their leader." Adrian smiled like a young boy for a brief second.

Frank led Adrian and Race through the main gate, past the tall, electrified fences with their guard towers and machine guns. Not a blade of grass grew in the area between the fences. As they moved through the grounds they passed several unguarded internal security points – areas that in the old days had required specialized credentials to enter. Those rules no longer seemed to apply. Jackrabbits wandered everywhere with their hunched backs and long, black-tipped ears, nimbly hopping out of the way at the last moment. When sitting, their long skinny forelegs supported their upper bodies as though on stilts, reminding Adrian somewhat of small kangaroos.

"Rafe Abram at your disposal, Mr. President," a tall gangly man said. He was in his late sixties, tall, stooped, and thin. "It is indeed a pleasure to meet you sir, but under somewhat strained circumstances, eh?"

"The pleasure is all mine, Mr. Abram, and please just call me 'Adrian.' We have a lot to discuss, and damn little time to discuss it. No sense wasting it on formalities. Can we get right to business?"

"Certainly, certainly. Let's get to it."

Frank interrupted. "Sir, do you need me here for this or should I get back to the men?"

"By all means Frank, get back to your men. Give Race a tour of the perimeter defenses. I'll brief you in a couple of hours on how we're going to set this up." Turning to the scientist he said, "Give me a quick rundown on the munitions and engineering facilities."

Rafe briefed him.

Thirty minutes later Adrian said, "So let me recap. There are thirty-nine buildings in the complex and they all have flat roofs. Stored underground you have over twelve-thousand nuclear pits from small tactical weapons on up to the great big bangers. These pits require extremely high explosives to trigger them and you have literally tons of that. You have a dream-team of engineers and the fabrication facilities are excellent. That about sum it up?"

"Pretty close, yes."

"Okay, here's what I want you to do..." Adrian outlined his plan. Half an hour later, Adrian asked. "Now, is this doable?"

"It is, but I have my doubts as to whether or not we can do it in the time we have. Engineers aren't exactly production people Adrian. They can design what you want quickly; building it is something else."

"You have the shop facilities to build them, and more than enough materials. I'll supply practical, experienced folks to help with the fabrication. There are people with a wide variety of skills in the militia we brought. Between your people and mine, I think we might pull it off."

"Okay, Adrian. Since time is the major constraint let's not waste any more of it. I'll assemble the engineers and scientists, you bring your people, we'll get them briefed en-masse, and turn them loose."

"I like the way you think, Rafe. Everyone outside this building in one hour?"

"Done."

An hour later and Adrian and Rafe were addressing the assembly. "Ladies and Gentlemen." Adrian began. "We are soon to be attacked by two very large, very determined, well-armed Chinese military groups. We estimate twelve-hundred soldiers, possibly more, with artillery. Their mission is to take Pantex. They'll be bringing their own scientists and engineers. When they take Pantex, they will assemble nuclear war heads and bombs, and bring in missiles and aircraft to deliver those war heads wherever they want to in our country. In short, taking Pantex means taking our country. This isn't just the most decisive battle in the Chinese invasion. This is the *entire point* of the invasion. This, right here, is the war.

"Terrain is on their side. Firepower is on their side. Numbers are on their side. Time, in fact, is on their side. But we have two things on our side: Motivation, and the fact that they need this facility intact when they take it. They have strong motivation, they've come thousands of miles through countless hardships to get here. They have no plans of leaving here alive unless they win. They will fight to the death because they cannot go home – there is no retreat for them.

"Our motivation is much stronger, though. This is our land, our country, our homes, our families on the line. In short, this is ours and they are not going to take it from us." Adrian paused for a moment as the crowd suddenly erupted into loud cheers. Adrian let them cheer themselves out, it was a release of tension that they badly needed.

"We have a plan. A plan that can certainly work, but only if we can implement it before they get here... and they are not far away. We have men and women fighting them, holding them back as long as they can. They are fighting, and dying at this very moment; dying in order to buy us minutes, hours, possibly a day.

"There may be other Chinese contingents on the way that we haven't spotted, approaching unhindered. We have to make the absolute utmost use of what time we have. There's no time for sleeping or eating or standing still. When you get your orders you must jump to it immediately, pursue it with the knowledge that your country, your life and the lives of those that you love depend on how fast you work. The plan is simple, its components are simple. I hate to say it in this crowd, but most of what happens next is *not* rocket science." Adrian paused as some in the crowd laughed, several scientists getting mildly poked in the ribs.

"So, do I have your full support? Will you work like you've never worked before?" Adrian's voice slowly rose as he spoke, ending on a crescendo. The crowd reacted, almost violently with a huge roar.

Adrian waited the couple of minutes it took them to settle down. "Okay then, I'll give you the overall plan, then each of you will be assigned your part in the mission. After that it will be up to you as individuals and as teams to make it happen."

Adrian spoke for another thirty minutes, outlining the plan and how it would be implemented. After he completed the outline the crowd went wild again. Now that they knew the plan, knew how it would work, they knew that it all depended on whether or not they were fast enough. They were as ready as any group of people ever had been. The team captains took the podium and began shouting out names, telling them where to assemble and what to bring with them.

Adrian stood back and watched, thought over the plan one more time, and knew it had a decent chance – if they could pull the elements together in time.

Adrian caught Rafe's eye, silently signaled him to meet him inside. As the doors closed, Adrian put a hand on Rafe's shoulder and said, "There's one more thing, Rafe. We have to have a fail-safe to keep the Chinese from gaining control. We have to set up a nuclear explosion that will take this plant completely out if we can't hold it."

Rafe looked startled then scared. "Adrian, it would kill every living thing for miles around, obviously including all of us."

Adrian didn't say anything, just watched and waited for Rafe to run through the scenarios. Finally, with a down-hearted shrug, he said, "Of course you are correct. It has to be done. I'll see to it myself."

"And keep it quiet, Rafe. I believe that everyone here would agree with this if it was laid out for them, but it won't be all that good for morale."

"I'll need help, two people. They are reliable, they won't talk after I explain it to them."

CHAPTER 19

"**H**OW'S THE WAR GOING ADMIRAL?" Adrian asked over the radio.

"Bad, Adrian. Very bad. We've got ships hitting the shores on both coasts at an alarming rate. There may be a hundred thousand Chinese troops on the ground right now, and more every day. It's really hard to say how many. The ports are under heavy attack, and we're running out of explosives boats. The Gulf of Mexico is one huge battle now, ships everywhere and more coming in by the minute. Your idea of staging attack boats from off-shore drilling rigs was excellent by the way, they've taken a heavy toll on the Chinese ships. But they'll run out of boats before long, too."

"Any engagement by the Chinese Navy yet?"

"None. They're sitting out there, waiting. Its eerie how you predicted that. I wish to hell they would attack already... I'd like to get our ships into action."

"Patience Admiral. Is there any good news?"

"Some. The militias in several places have taken on the Chinese ground troops and are pretty much holding their own, following the guerrilla tactics you laid out. Our reports are sporadic at best, though; we may not be hearing from the militias that got into deep trouble. So I don't really know at this point.

Most of our aircraft are down. We have to save what we have for naval reconnaissance. How about you? Any good news there?"

"Some. We have a reasonable chance to defend the plant here, assuming we can get everything together in time. They'll never take this plant, though, even if we lose."

"What are you saying, Adrian? What does that mean?"

"It means just what I said, Admiral. If it comes to it... they won't get our nukes."

There was a long pause as the Admiral considered what Adrian was saying.

"Adrian, you must leave there immediately. Get to someplace safer. Hell...go back to Corpus Christi. Bad as it is there, it's better than where you are. This country needs you to lead it, not die for it."

"It's too late Admiral, even if I wanted to leave I can't. I couldn't leave here for my own personal safety and still have enough self-integrity left to lead. If I die, this is as good a place and as good a cause as there ever will be. Just be certain that I know I'm doing what needs to be done. A martyr might be just what this country needs anyway." Adrian said with a chuckle. "Martyrs have no faults, while live leaders have plenty of them."

Adrian spent every moment going from group to group, praising the men and women as he watched them furiously working at their assignments. Hour by hour he was seeing it come together, one piece at a time. Each team was focused on accomplishing their goals, building their items. On top of the buildings other teams were reinforcing roof structures to accommodate added weight, while still others set up transits for measuring distances. In the underground structures, teams were busy assembling their delicate projects. It was like walking through an ant hive where all the ants were on speed.

Deep underground, the most delicate of operations were taking place. Adrian was cheering on a group as a runner approached him. "Sir, enemy spotted coming in, you're wanted topside."

Adrian followed the runner as they literally ran up stairwell after stairwell to reach the top of the highest building. When they reached the roof, the runner pointed breathlessly to a group of four spotters gathered at the roof's edge with binoculars. Adrian asked them "What and where?"

"There sir. Coming in from the north, a convoy about a mile out. They appear to have stopped..., been stopped about five minutes sir."

Adrian took the proffered binoculars and took a long look. "You're right, it's a Chinese convoy. A big one. Damned if I know where they came from, we had no reports of anything from the north. Doesn't matter though cause there they are, big as Dallas. Send for Rafe and Matcher, get them up here, *pronto*."

Ten minutes later Adrian told Rafe, "Get whatever equipment is ready and place them on those roofs over there." Adrian pointed to three buildings near the northern perimeter. "Fast as you can...whatever you have." Rafe immediately left to implement the order.

Adrian turned to Matcher. "Frank, either they're

going to wait for the other two contingents for a unified attack, or they'll begin the attack without them. We'll know shortly which. I'd rather they waited, giving us more time, but we'll deal with whatever happens best we can. Now, if you were them and you began the attack, how would you do it?"

"Sir, I would have my artillery concentrate on the fence line. My first objective would be blowing away the perimeter fences. I'd have my infantry move forward under cover of the artillery fire. When they're close in I'd stop the artillery, advance my infantry, and charge in, take the perimeter and set up a base of operations for a building to building fight."

"You got it in one, Lieutenant. Now, how would you defend against that attack, assuming it's just you and your troops to work with?"

"I can only see one way, sir. Hold back from the perimeter until the infantry charge, then charge out to meet them head-on."

"That's what they expect Frank. Not much else we can do... except to place half your troops in reserve and bring them out on either side of the Chinese just before they reach the fence line. Use the heavy, belt-fed machine guns from inside the perimeter, set them up on those roofs over there. That will give them three fronts to fight and their artillery won't be able to fire without hitting their own men, so they'll be on their own. We'll pour heavy fire down into them from the high ground while hitting them from three sides. It gives us a better chance than tackling them head to head. Get your troops ready, Frank."

"Yes sir." Frank saluted and trotted off at double time.

Adrian continued to watch the far-off convoy while waiting for the troops to move into place. After half an hour, Rafe returned. "We have three of your creations on the way, with twenty-six total shots ready, Adrian. Half an hour to get them set up. It's going to be ragged, though; we're working strictly on theory here, with no time for field-testing anything."

"Maximum range?"

"Half a mile outside, and two or three hundred yards on the short side. We can reach past those outbuildings handily enough."

"Sniper shields?"

"We have enough for this operation. More being made quickly, everyone moving as fast as they can."

"Good enough for now." Adrian replied. "They may or may not attack until the other elements get here. They may or may not attack on the north side, they could swing around from any side at the last moment. Get everything we have up here as fast as we can, we need to have full deployment by morning. They may make a night attack so make sure the perimeter lights are all active. They'll probably have night vision equipment, which is something we don't have. Those lights may be our life for as long as they last. Can we have the lasers ready for tonight?"

"Six of them in total, half will be ready by night fall."

"Any of them ready now?"

"Two."

"Go ahead and bring them up, they'll do their job as well in the daytime won't they?"

"Certainly."

"Rafe, I want you to know that you're doing a damn fine job, far better than I could have hoped for."

"Well hell, Adrian, us desk jockeys can move when we have to."

"I'm seeing that. Your people aren't just brilliant, they're tough as nails when the chips are down. Now, please go see that everything moves as fast as possible."

An hour later, Adrian was watching the installation of the machines and powerful lasers Rafe's scientists had modified. Race came up on the roof.

"Adrian," she said, "Frank asked me to tell you that the ground troops are lined out and ready. They can move to any perimeter quickly, although the heavy machine guns on the roofs would take a bit longer. We've also gotten radio reports from our counter-convoy teams. Both have had significant effect on the convoy's speeds. They're estimating that the rest of the Chinese will arrive mid-day tomorrow, and at only sixty-five percent strength."

"Good news, then. Did they focus on taking out the artillery?"

"Yes sir, they did, and they've been pretty effective at it. They report heavy damage to those; they estimate that about fifty-percent are probably out of commission."

"Excellent. Tell them to continue to focus on the artillery for whatever actions they can still take. Slowing them down still helps, but reducing their artillery will help more now. By noon tomorrow we'll be as ready as we're going to get. The time they've bought us has been tremendous, be sure to let them know. How many casualties have we taken?"

"Minor, because they've followed your orders to hit and run fast. They're still over ninety-five percent operational. They'll be here to kick the Chinese hard from behind, too, when the time comes."

There was a short pause as they watched the equipment being set up.

"Adrian, how did you come up with this idea? Do you think it's really going to work?"

"From reading and watching television back in the old days. It'll work for its purpose, of that much I'm sure. I'm also sure they won't be expecting anything like it, and that element of surprise is going to double the effectiveness of it, at least for a little while. Ultimately it may come down to a hand-to-hand battle among the buildings. What we have to do is eliminate as many of their ground troops as we can before we get to that point."

Race left to follow up on her orders. Alone with his thoughts, Adrian looked like a statue staring out at the vast flat plains. The sun was getting low, lighting up the left side of his face with a glowing red hue. He cast a long shadow across the roof's edge and out across the prairie land below.

All night long, Adrian pitched in –moving equipment to the roof tops, and encouraging exhausted men and women to keep the level of effort at a fever pitch. The perimeter lights had been turned off and work was performed by moonlight only. There was a constant shuffle of people coming and going on the roofs, materials being carried up by hand, assembly teams working frantically in the near-dark to complete their tasks. It was a bizarre scene, surreal under the moonlight. There was the constant sound of shuffling feet, large pieces of steel being dragged across roofs, people talking in low voices to each other with the occasional voice raised in frustration or sudden warnings to others when something heavy moved that wasn't supposed to move.

Adrian kept the pressure up by example. Never once was he seen resting or standing still. Constant motion, constant attention to detail, continuous encouragement to those around him. Thirty-six hours of hard, fast labor, no sleep, and no time for meals was taking a heavy toll on everyone. Not only physical toll, but a mental toll. Stress was rampant from lack of sleep, lack of rest and the constant challenge of keeping moving because the enemy was gathering around them, an enemy superior in numbers and firepower. An enemy better trained and more rested. Everyone was near to dropping, but they not only pushed on, they pushed on at high speed.

The night gradually wore on, the moon slowly traversing the sky overhead, changing the shadow patterns as the defenses were put into place. Eventually the moon disappeared several hours before the sun began to brighten the eastern sky. Dawn crept forward, until suddenly the sun crested the flat horizon with its leading edge. In only a matter of minutes it cleared the horizon and Adrian could clearly see all of the work that had taken shape during the darkness. It was an impressive sight. Never before had he seen so many do so much with so little in such a short period of time. By the time the sun was twenty degrees above the horizon they were finished.

Adrian called out in a huge voice, one intended to be heard by every person on every roof. He called out an inarticulate satisfaction, a primal triumphant battle cry that soared through the hearts of everyone on the roofs. It was a genuine heartfelt satisfaction for their supreme efforts, their driving will to get this done. Tears sprang to many eyes, men's and women's. A heroic effort had taken place, one that would live long in their memories, stories that would be passed down the generations, fill the new history books to be written – if any of them survived the coming ordeal to tell it. And that ordeal would begin in a few short hours. The other two convoys were now in sight.

CHAPTER 20

ADRIAN ORDERED MOST OF THE militia and each firing team to stand down and sleep. He wanted them as rested as they could be when the battle started. Most dropped where they were, on roof tops or on the ground, and collapsed into deep troubled, desperately needed sleep. Everyone else kept working until each station was complete, ammunition at the ready, and ready to fire. Then one by one they went into the air-conditioned buildings and lay down wherever there was space to stretch out.

Adrian paced the roof, watching the three Chinese contingents, waiting for them to attack. Two hours went by with little sign of movement. Then, at precisely noon the trucks began to fan out. Race asked to be relieved to fight on the ground, and Adrian reluctantly agreed, then called for everyone else to be woken up immediately. Groggily the firing teams stood, many rubbing their eyes, then staring out at the Chinese before taking up their own positions. The men and women below were awakened as well, many of them were relief for the firing teams in case of injury or death.

It started with heavy sniper fire. The Chinese had optics, and had watched the mad scramble during the night and early morning hours. A four-sided steel box had been set up for Adrian and his radio team, two-inch steel plates tack-welded in place. The plate iron would stop everything the Chinese snipers could throw, as long as a bullet didn't come through a view port. If one did it would ricochet relentlessly inside the steel box. As the sniper fire began, there was very little sound except the sharp pinging of bullets hitting steel plate. The sound of the gunshots slowly drifted in afterwards, faint from the distance.

Under the cover of sniper fire, the Chinese rolled their artillery into place. Eight from the north, four from the west, and three from the south. The artillery teams were well drilled. Each piece fired a test round, then rapidly adjusting their aim, the heavy pounding started in earnest. The fences on three sides took a deliberate beating, being blown up in large shreds from the explosive impacts. Ten minutes of continuous artillery fire and the fences were gone, but the pounding continued as the infantry troops began moving rapidly across the open ground. It was a simple, three-pronged attack, following the pattern that Frank had so clearly stated. Under cover of the artillery barrage, the infantry teams moved rapidly forward, easily covering the flat, exposed, unchallenged ground.

When the first infantry man crossed the three-thousand foot mark Adrian order the firing teams to hold for another five-hundred yards. They didn't have to hold long. When the enemy reached the twenty-five hundred foot mark Adrian picked up the radio and said "Fire at will."

Race and Frank lay behind one of the many barricades hastily built during the night. The artillery shelling of the fence line was a continuous roar of sound, blinding lights, and flying debris. They watched intently, waiting for the shelling to stop. When it finally did, they knew the Chinese soldiers would be coming within seconds. It was nerve-wracking.

They could not see beyond the haze of dirt and debris. Then from far out in the field, a huge flash of light momentarily penetrated through the dust cloud. Simultaneously a shockwave hit, making the ground jump. The pressure wave was fiercely intense. Then another, and a ragged series following the first two. Race was stunned by the concussion waves rolling across them. She tried shouting to Frank "Adrian said they were super-explosives but damn, I had no idea." Frank pointed to his ear and shook his head to indicate he couldn't hear. Race already knew he couldn't, she hadn't even heard herself.

They grinned at each other then returned to watching the perimeter. The shelling and the huge yellowish-white blooms of light from the roof-top launched explosives continued for another five minutes, seeming an eternity to them. The explosives stopped, then suddenly the artillery barrage stopped as well. With ears ringing, Race and Frank jumped up from their prone positions and ran to the fence line followed by their fire teams. Spreading out along the fence line, the defenders took cover in the still smoking craters left from the artillery barrage.

Adrian watched closely as two types of machines went into action. Half of them were compressed air firing tubes, loaded with high explosives wrapped in shrapnel and containing an altimeter firing device. There were several loud whooshing sounds as the air cannons hammered the explosive charge high into the air. These explosive rounds were made from very high explosives – the components used to trigger nuclear pits – and were far more powerful than anything that could be obtained anywhere else. The shrapnel was made from whatever scrap metal could be found and crammed into service; short pieces of chain and individual chain links, scrap iron cut into inch-long pieces.

The second type of machines were trebuchets. Simple to build, simple to operate, and with almost as much range as the air-powered tubes. They used the same ammunition. The explosives arced up high above the enemy soldiers, then cascaded downwards. When they were twenty feet above the ground they exploded sending huge shock waves, and shrapnel flying at supersonic speeds, into the waves of Chinese infantry. The first few shots were somewhat ragged, the teams had only been able to do mock practice at loading and firing, but they swiftly grew more profficient, raining down a lethal hell-fire on the enemy below.

Adrian, using the radio said, "Deploy lasers."

He watched as the laser beams swept back and forth across the enemy lines, creating additional fear and distraction and most importantly of all – temporary blindness in many of the soldiers, buying the defenders time to reload the air cannons and trebuchets. The air cannons took time to recharge, but each could be fired at a rate of once every ninety-seconds. The trebuchets were a little faster, but not much.

The Chinese lines stalled for several minutes because of the brutal aerial assault, then slowly the leaders got the men moving again and they charged on ahead in spite of taking horrendous casualties, an event they had not expected in their wildest dreams. They had been told that the facility was defended by a small group of poorly trained ground troops; they had no idea what was hitting them, but it was worse than a living hell. Their discipline was the only thing that kept them moving forward. When they reached the outbuildings, Adrian ordered them to be exploded with the pre-placed explosives in and around them taking out more of the Chinese soldiers and leaving them with no cover.

The Chinese's artillery stopped as their infantry closed in. Now the troop surge was in range of the rooftop machine guns and Adrian ordered them to open up. The front ranks had crossed under the shortest range of the contrived artillery on the roofs. Militia rushed to the fence line, finding artillery craters they could use for cover, laying down withering fire into the advancing infantry who had no cover to shelter behind. The Chinese were taking extremely heavy fire and were being cut down in large numbers. Only a few made it to the fence line, and those were killed quickly.

For a moment there was nothing to see but smoke

and swirling dust. Then the heavy machine guns above them opened up, signaling the approach of the enemy infantry soldiers. Frank opened fire, shooting beyond where he could see. The rest of the militia followed his cue and began firing also.

The first thing Race saw was a falling soldier. He seemed to fall out of the dust, just appearing in view. He hit the ground like a loose sack of meat, dead before he fell. Then there were hundreds of soldiers, staggering forward. Some were firing, most were not. They staggered almost blindly forward, their senses shocked by the massive concussive forces they'd been hit by. Several were clawing at their eyes, blinded to differing extents by the lasers that had swept across their eyes.

The militia continued to fire, but now that they could see their targets they were taking deliberate aim. The Chinese kept coming, but they were no longer effective fighting men, they were moving forward blindly, without understanding. The militia cut them down by the hundreds and yet they still kept coming. Now the ones in the second wave had to stumble over the bodies of the men who had died in front of them, slowing them down in their forward movement. Between the roof-top machine guns and the ground fire, the Chinese were taking a terrible beating.

But their numbers were too much for the bullets to stop entirely and soon the Chinese were on top of them. Race shot a soldier in the face when he was only ten feet away, then another and still they kept coming. The lines engaged in hand to hand combat. Race had run her clip dry, and with no time to put another one in she was face to face with two men. Pulling her knife from the belt sheath she flew at them slashing and stabbing. Out of the periphery of her awareness she knew that Frank and the entire front line were in the same situation.

The militia gradually gained the upper hand. They were severely outnumbered by the Chinese, but the Chinese were shell shocked, moving almost in slow motion, disoriented by the devastating bombardment they'd somehow managed to survive. This gave the militia the edge. The Chinese onslaught slowed, then stopped altogether. Then suddenly they retreated, running away as fast as they could. The militia stood still momentarily, then quickly regaining their own wits they realized they'd fought forward, not just holding their ground but advancing. They retreated back to the fence line, loaded their weapons and began to take care of their wounded. Race noticed that her rifle was slung over her shoulder and she had her six gun in her hand. She did not remember making the switch. Huge concussive blasts resumed as the retreating Chinese once again crossed through the range of the flying explosives.

Adrian directed the ground battle from the roof top as the battle raged for twenty minutes. Using radio, he directed the different militia groups to attack or pull back as conditions on the ground warranted. Finally, what was left of the Chinese withdrew, turning their backs to the heavy small arms fire to run, continuing to be cut down as they ran. As they ran through the trebuchet and air tube range again more explosives were launched into them. By the time they were out of range, only a handful of Chinese soldiers remained.

At that moment the militia that had followed behind the south and west components attacked. They were there to keep the artillery from opening up again and aiming for the compound itself, something Adrian was sure was against their standing orders. But they were thousands of miles away from their dictators and could easily disobey those orders – it was obvious they weren't going to take the facility the way they had planned, and they could not go home. They might decide that their only chance would be to flatten the compound's buildings, along with the defenders, then pick through the rubble. They would know that they would still find much of the materials they sought underground.

While the western and southern Chinese artillery teams were kept pinned down by the militias in two places, the northern component wasn't under the same constraint. This is where Adrian's final surprise came in – on wings. Adrian's last request to Captain Morgan had been for a gunship. It had been a chancy, last-minute thing; Adrian hadn't known if it would make it in time, or even if it would make it at all. But Morgan had come through. Coming over the horizon was an AC-131 gunship. The gunship quickly came into play over the northern component.

Seeming to stand on one wing, it flew in a tight circle and delivered rapid-fire killing blows to the Chinese. Firing 40mm cannons and 105mm cannons rapidly into the convoy and artillery, the Chinese were ripped to shreds in less than two minutes. The aircraft then proceeded to wipe out the other two components. It then flew over the compound, dipped its wings, and flew off to the west and landed on the highway.

Everyone was cheering, hugging, and dancing. People were pouring onto the roof in celebration. The militia on the ground were moving through the enemy combatants, making sure none remained alive.

Adrian got on the radio and said, "Everyone in front of the building in thirty minutes, and I mean every single person."

Turning to Race who had come back onto the roof to report he asked, "Casualties?"

"Yes sir. First report is forty dead, sixty wounded, ten critically."

"Damn," was all Adrian said.

Standing in front of the crowd, most of whom were still cheering and dancing, Adrian began to speak. "First let me report that we took casualties, mostly on the ground but some from sniper fire. Today we lost good friends. Brave men and women who paid with their lives and their blood to protect all of us. I think a prayer is in order." Pointing to one of his militia buddies, Matt, blacksmith, inventor, militiaman, and Preacher, Adrian asked "Would you mind, Matt?"

After Matt's short but beautiful prayer, Adrian spoke again. "Would someone go and lower the flag to half-mast please?" Two men quickly did and Adrian stood at attention and saluted.

Then Adrian said, "You. All of you. You worked harder than anyone I've ever seen work before. By the strength of your will you turned certain defeat into total victory. This is a moment in history that will echo through the ages. Your names will be remembered. Generations from now people will talk about you with awe... and gratitude... for you have saved your countrymen from an overall defeat at the hands of the Chinese who would have used these nuclear weapons against us. I firmly believe that this is the critical turning point in this war. As word is broadcast across the land of what you've done here, your actions, your victory will inspire all of the other militias. They will fight harder, be braver, and have more will to win than anything else in the world could have inspired.

"You didn't just save your own lives. You saved countless lives by denying this arsenal to our enemy. Be proud of what you have accomplished. You just sent the clearest signal possible to the Chinese empire that *they will not take our land!*"

The crowd had fallen deathly silent up to that point, but with those words they erupted into a cheer that could be heard for miles around as it echoed across the land and over the bodies of the enemy bodies lying on the prairie.

CHAPTER 21

PANTEX SUPPLIED FUEL FROM ITS reserves for the AC-130; the gunship had used nearly all of its fuel to reach Pantex from Florida. It would not be returning to Florida, but to Corpus Christi, carrying Adrian, Race, Frank, and the Texas Rangers, crammed into it when it lifted off. They circled the battlefield from eight-thousand feet and Adrian looked down. Pantex was in good shape, but spread out on three sides of it were perhaps two thousand bodies; thicker near the plant perimeter. Large black scorched earth marks indicated where the primitively launched, technologically advanced bombs had exploded.

More troops were being mobilized to set up a robust and permanent defense at Pantex. Artillery and other tactically useful weapons would be sent in as well. Adrian didn't expect to fight another battle for Pantex, but the downside if he was wrong was too horrendous to not take every precaution.

Over the intercom the pilot said, "Mr. President, it's an amazing feat. Coupling primitive technology with advanced technology that way. Not to mention how rapidly it was deployed."

"We had incredible human resources," said Adrian. "Scientists, engineers, and soldiers working together with the kind of tools and explosives they had at hand is something I would never want to face. If the Chinese had wanted to destroy the plant instead of capturing it whole we would never had had a chance, not in a million years. That was our ace in the hole – and you were the other ace."

"My pleasure to be of service, sir," replied the pilot.

The plane banked right and headed for Fort Brazos, where Adrian and the Rangers would be offloaded and return to their normal duties. For the first time in several weeks, Adrian would spend the night with Linda before proceeding on to Corpus Christi.

The entire village was gathered near the bridge over the Brazos River on FM-2114 where the AC-131 landed. It was two miles from Fort Brazos, the closest place they could land, yet it looked like every man, woman, and child had turned out to welcome the returning heroes. Linda led the charge to the aircraft's door and everyone was cheering and clapping when the door opened and Adrian stepped out. He paused for a moment to wave, then lunged for Linda, grabbed her up in a bear hug, and whirled her around in circles. Between the winding down engines and the crowd's cheering, Adrian couldn't have spoken loud enough for Linda to hear him, but his hug did enough talking for the moment.

If anything the crowd grew even louder as Race and the Rangers stepped off the plane. Eventually everyone moved back to the village, leaving a well-armed group behind to guard the aircraft. The ten-man crew was treated like royalty. The details of the

Pantex battle were widely known already, including the gunship crew's part in the battle.

When things quieted down Linda asked, "How long can you stay?"

"Just overnight. We may have reached the tipping point in this war, but I'm not sure of that and even if I were, there's still a lot of heavy fighting still to be done."

"I'll take every second I can get darling, every single second is a treasure beyond price."

The afternoon was filled with celebrations and speeches. It was an odd celebration though. The villagers knew that Adrian needed to spend every minute he could in privacy with Linda, so they shooed the couple into their home as soon as they arrived. Then they gathered in front of the house and carried on with speeches and toasts and more than a little drinking while the couple reconnected inside.

"Straight to the bedroom, Adrian, I'm going to give you a proper hero's welcome."

"Damn, Linda, I'm not sure I can carry on properly with all that noise outside!" Adrian replied with a grin. She quickly showed him he could.

Later that night, when the celebrants had moved on into the village, Adrian sent for his kitchen cabinet. Matt, Perry, Tim and Race sat at the kitchen table with a glowing Linda and Adrian.

"The reason I asked you here," Adrian began, "is I need your advice. Pantex is not the only nuclear storage facility we have; there are about a dozen other locations that hold ready-to-go nukes. My concern is that the Chinese are also aware of these other locations. Pantex holds the largest number of nuclear pits along with a sizeable amount of active war heads, but every site is a potential target. It may be that the Chinese land forces have those in mind. If even one is captured we're back to square one, losing the war.

"While I feel certain that we will win with our present strategy, it's going to take too long, there's too much exposure and too many opportunities for them to get one of those nuke storage sites. I've sent out orders to beef up security at each of them, but defense is a poor security option when offense is available. What I'm thinking is that our best defense now is to end this war quickly... and that means we have to radically change strategy. The final decision is on my shoulders, but I need to hear every pro and con you guys can come up with. The burden of the consequences could be enormous, and I don't want anyone at this table to feel the slightest shred of that burden. This will be my decision alone – remember that as we go through this discussion. Please, do not hold back any thought you have...no matter how odd or silly it may seem to you."

Adrian stopped talking, looking each one directly in the eyes for a moment.

Matt said, "Okay, we got it. Now what're you thinking of?"

Adrian laid it out for them. The discussion went on until the sun came up and Adrian had to leave for Corpus Christi. As he boarded the AC-131 his mind was made up. The war was about to change, radically.

Adrian returned to the ship and was met by Captain

Morgan and the full complement of the carrier's crew, turned out in full dress uniforms, and arranged in formation on the carrier's deck. All hands, except for the necessary duty crews, were on deck. He was given a military hero's welcome with loud cheering and hats flying high into the air.

Embarrassed, Adrian turned to Morgan and said, "Jesus, Morgan, was this really necessary?"

"Yes, sir," Morgan replied simply.

"I really don't need this kind of hurrahing, Morgan."

"No sir, I know you don't. But *they* do. They're so damn proud of your weirdly awesome stand at Pantex that they're about to burst. If they don't get a chance to let you know how they feel... well they'll be cheated, sir."

"Oh," was all Adrian could say for a moment. "I hadn't thought of that."

"It's not just them either, sir. It's every man, woman, and child in this country. It's as though the Alamo was fought all over again except this time the good guys won. Not only won, but won heroically and by using tactics that no one in their right mind would have thought of. It was a brilliant victory, sir, just fucking brilliant if you'll pardon my French, and everyone is beyond proud of you and the men and women at Pantex. It's become a new battle cry, sir. Men charging into battle all over this country are shouting '*Remember Pantex.*'"

"Seriously? They're yelling that?"

"Yes sir, it spread like wildfire. You'll have to get used to this kind of welcome, sir, it's going to happen wherever you go. My advice, which I know you don't need, is to not just let it happen, but to encourage it. Soldiers need more than a good cause to fight for sir, they need to believe in their leader. They need to believe that the man leading this war *can* win it, *will* win it. Sir, think back to when you were in the Army and going out on missions. You wanted to believe that the powers that be knew exactly what they were doing, even if it didn't make sense to you – especially when it *didn't* make sense to you. When you believed they knew what they were doing, you fought better, harder, and with confidence. When you didn't believe that, when you had doubts about your orders, you weren't as effective. It's the same for everyone, sir."

"Well, Morgan, when you're right you're right. Carry on with the celebration, but when it's over I need to see you in my cabin and get an uplink to the Admirals."

Three hours later Adrian completed the conference call with the Admiral and Rutherford. The call had taken over an hour. Adrian listened to the pros and cons the Admirals and Morgan had elucidated. Each had already been gone over by his kitchen cabinet and Adrian considered all of them. He was as confident as he could be in his new strategy, and well aware of the possible consequences. The trio had, in the end, agreed with him. Encrypted and encoded messages were flying around the country at that very moment, organizing and implementing the first stage of the plan.

Adrian was exhausted. He'd had only a few hours of sleep since the beginning stages of the Pantex battle. He'd caught a short nap on each leg of the journey back on the AC-131. He hadn't gotten any sleep at Fort Brazos. "Morgan, I'm going to sleep for eight hours, do not disturb me unless there's an emergency."

"Yes, sir. And if I may say so, a damn good idea. You're about to fall over." Morgan left, pulling the door quietly closed behind him. Adrian was asleep before Morgan was out of the cabin.

Eight hours later Adrian awakened himself by his internal alarm clock. He was aware that the crew would probably have let him sleep around the clock despite his orders, they wouldn't have disturbed his rest for anything less than a total crisis. But Adrian had slept as much as he dared, time was of the essence and he had to get back to Pantex to get things started personally.

By that evening he was landing on a heli-pad on top of one of the buildings at Pantex. Coming in he had looked down at the battlefield. The Chinese soldiers were being buried in a mass grave, a caterpillar pushing dirt over the hole, forming a large mound of dirt that would settle some, but would be visible on the flat plain for centuries, possibly the tallest landmark for fifty miles. The trebuchets and air tubes were still in place on the roof tops. Simple machines, they could withstand the weather for years with only minor maintenance. The lasers that had been so effective had been removed, too delicate to be left exposed.

Once again he was given a hero's welcome. As Morgan had suggested, he went along with it. When it was over he and Rafe retired to Rafe's office for privacy. They had a lot to talk about.

CHAPTER 22

"CERTAINLY WE CAN DO THAT, Mr. President," said Rafe, scratching his head. "But as before, time is the critical factor. How many do you need? I know we're behind already, so I won't ask when you need them. I can get you twenty... maybe thirty in a week."

"That'll be a good start, but can you get me ten in three days? I have transport on the way here ready to distribute them within two days after that. Ten will give us a good start, and with a ton of luck they may be enough. Ultimately I'll want two hundred, as fast as you can churn them out."

"Once we get an assembly line set up and running, we can assemble them quickly. I'd say it will take us about three weeks to make two hundred; remember we have limited personnel capable of this kind of work, and I'm talking full court press with them. If I may suggest... I think if you were to meet with them and explain why you want these... the urgency of the need... it would go a long way towards motivating them to their maximum effort. They're still exhausted, you know. We all are."

"I'll be more than happy to. Would you go ahead and gather them up?"

"Give me thirty minutes."

Adrian remained at Pantex for the next four days, and was on-site when the transport planes arrived. He looked them over and shook his head at the motley assemblage of the aircraft that were still running.

Every day the number of flying aircraft in the country became smaller. Lack of maintenance mechanics and lack of new parts were taking a heavy toll. Before the CME collapsed the world's technologies, Adrian had never given a thought to the massive effort it took to keep airplanes flying – it seemed the more complex the aircraft, the faster it became useless. By this time, very few military aircraft could be put in the air. However, the simple single-engine, fixed-wheel private aircraft were still holding up fairly well. They were small and slow and they didn't carry a lot, but they tended to still work because they were simple to work on, and there had been tens of thousands of them that could be cannibalized for parts.

Adrian was on the roof looking over the small aircraft parked nearby. He turned to Rafe, "You know if these weren't so damn easy to shoot down we could really use them. But they are just too slow and have no defenses. For them to be effective they would have to fly in low and slow. The Bed-Check-Charlie system of warfare won't cut it. Way too easy to shoot down. Every one of these is now a major transport asset, no point in getting them shot down.

"Rafe, you've done tremendous work. I'm heading out with the cargo, probably won't get to come back here for a long time." Adrian reached out to shake Rafe's hand. Rafe extended his and when they clasped Adrian pulled the older man to him in a brief hug. "Thank you Rafe. I won't waste your efforts."

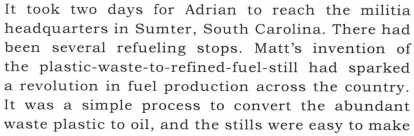

It took two days for Adrian to reach the militia headquarters in Sumter, South Carolina. There had been several refueling stops. Matt's invention of the plastic-waste-to-refined-fuel-still had sparked a revolution in fuel production across the country. It was a simple process to convert the abundant waste plastic to oil, and the stills were easy to make from scrap metal. It took hard work to harvest the plastics and run the stills, but hard work was no longer a rare phenomenon in the country – it took hard work to survive, and the only people left from the CME disaster, were by definition, survivors.

At each fuel stop, there was an enthusiastic, cheering crowd waiting for Adrian, people coming from miles around to see him. The crowd that greeted him when he arrived in Sumter was larger than those he'd seen at the fuel stops. To Adrian's dismay, he wasn't getting used to the welcoming crowds. He'd thought that in time it would be easier to deal with, yet he was still as discomfited each time as much as he had been the first time.

After the crowd began to disburse Adrian went into the building used as headquarters. It was a small building that had once been a private residence before being converted into a boutique office building. It stirred memories of one of the homes he'd lived in growing up. After a brief moment, Adrian shook off the nostalgia, and addressed the militia's leaders.

"Gentlemen, you no doubt know why I'm here."

Nods all around assured him they did know. "Please brief me on the situation on the ground."

Twelve hours later, Adrian was standing on a ridge top in North Carolina, looking down on a Chinese invasion force a mile away. The Chinese were moving south, following Highway 77. They were two miles north of the intersection with Highway 34. The militia leader, Larry Bowman, said, "We'll have a good view from here sir. We have five minutes."

Adrian picked up his radio microphone and said, "Admiral, I've always admired this quote. It's from way, way back, and has particular meaning for us now. In five minutes you will *'Cry havoc and let slip the dogs of war!'*"

"Mr. President, that is a most particularly appropriate phrase. Our ships are in position and ready to release total and utter havoc on the enemy. The other three land sites are prepared to simultaneously launch with you. The Chinese emperor will get your message loud and clear, sir, very loud and very clear."

Adrian hung up the radio and looked at his watch. "Larry," he said to the militiaman, "you are about to make history. What you are about to see will be something else entirely from anything you've ever seen before."

"Time to put on the goggles, sir."

Adrian took another long look at the Chinese below. Intelligence had studied them thoroughly; there were three thousand men down there, almost three hundred trucks carrying not only men, but helicopters, tanks, artillery and missile batteries. Inwardly he shuddered at the destruction he was about to unleash on them, most of them would die without knowing they had died, gone in a blink.

But they came here, here to our home, to kill our people, take over our land, use us like slaves. We'll send them to Hell in a blind fury for that. With that thought Adrian slipped the goggles down over his eyes.

Two seconds later he saw the white-hot flares of light through the dark glass, briefly lighting the up scene to a point where everything went white. When the light dimmed again, only seconds later, Adrian ripped the goggles off and looked.

He saw two small mushroom clouds forming at the third points of the column. Fire already raged on both sides of the road in the thick trees. Where before there had been an orderly march of military machinery, there was now chaos. Two large smoking craters with a clear area of several hundred yards and then a debris field of trucks and bodies. Total carnage lay below him. Carnage he had sought, mass death he had worked hard to create.

There was no sense of satisfaction for Adrian, only a grim belief that this had become necessary, and a realization that he personally would never be the same again. Something he had always liked about himself had died with the twin tactical-nuclear blasts.

Adrian raised the microphone.

Within moments in California and in Florida the scene was repeated as low-yield tactical nuclear weapons were deployed against the invading Chinese. In the Pacific, the Atlantic and the Gulf of

Mexico North American Naval forces opened up on Chinese Navy fleets. Missiles flew through the air at surface ships and submarines launched torpedoes at Chinese submarines and surface ships. *Havoc* had been the launch code, and havoc had been launched. In a matter of hours, the Chinese fleets were badly crippled. Within two weeks they would be completely destroyed.

The Chinese Navy was not unsophisticated, they delivered some serious blows of their own, sinking six American ships. But those losses, hard as they were to accept, were mild in comparison to what the Chinese received.

More tactical nuclear devices were being deployed every day, to be put into use as soon as they arrived at their destinations. Adrian was confident now, estimating two weeks until the war could be declared won on both ground and sea.

Three days later, Adrian was once again on the carrier at Corpus Christi, and on the radio with the Admiral.

"Adrian, the Chinese Emperor has made contact and asked to speak with you. Interested?"

"I am now. It saves me from calling him, a small victory in itself. We'll give it a try... make sure we have our own translator listening in. Better record it, too."

"Call you back when it's arranged."

Adrian was surprised at how quickly the call came back. "Twenty minutes from now, Adrian."

"Make sure you and Rutherford listen in, Morgan

will be here with me, listening. Will we have an interpreter on the line?"

Morgan replied, "We have one here on the ship, sir; she's perfectly fluent in all the dialects. One of our best intelligence officers, sir."

"Alright, gentlemen. I have an idea of what's he's going to try. It could get very interesting very fast."

The voice coming from the radio's speakers was as clear as if it was coming from the next room. Emperor Xao said in perfect English, "President Hunter, I must congratulate you on your courage and ingenuity. You resisted much better than I expected. As you would say 'my hat's off to you.' You are quite the unconventional warrior. I've enjoyed watching you maneuver – brilliant strategy, and your ever-evolving tactics have been a delight! Trebuchets! Completely and totally unexpected! Who else would have *ever* thought of that?"

The Emperor continued, "I know you believe you've won the war, but in fact you have only fought a small and meaningless battle. You have actually *lost* the war. Your small victory doesn't matter. That was just the easy way I chose to use first. After all, why use a smashing blow when only a small push may be required? But for the unfortunate circumstance of you, with your unconventional thinking, personally leading the war, a small push would have sufficed. You have resisted that small push brilliantly. But I'm getting bored with this small business and I have important things to attend to, so I'll get to the finish quickly. Total surrender now or look up into the skies at your country's complete destruction in say…twelve hours?" The voice was smooth, polished, a timbre of arrogant confidence arrived at after a lifetime of victories and no losses.

Adrian glanced at Morgan whose expression was stunned, shock in his eyes.

Adrian smiled and winked at Morgan. Then he replied, deliberately forgoing a formal response, "Xao, you're a real hoot. You're over there on your knees, shaking like a dog shitting peach pits." Adrian glanced at Morgan again. Morgan was now showing total shock. "No sir, I've got to hand it to you. Your war strategy wasn't so hot, but you have some giant balls to think I'd buy that line of bullshit. No, not balls... arrogance. You've been sitting in your ivory tower too long, son, so let me tell you how it is.

"You send your nukes over and ours will be coming at you in the same second. You know that. Only we have a lot more of them, and richer targets to boot. What are you going to hit over here? Big cities? There's hardly anyone in them; Hit the oil refineries? Hell, most of them aren't working now and never will be. Most of our people are oil independent you know, we can do just fine without it. So what's left? Nothing. We're in the unique position that you can't destroy our infrastructure because we don't have any we're using. But what can *we* target?

"Oh let's see... cities with millions of people in them. Your capital of course, all of your military installations, shipyards, and there's that big dam isn't there? We can hit all of them, we have more than enough bombs for every target you offer. We're talking a complete and final destruction of the Chinese Empire, ending how many thousands of years of rule? We'll survive, you won't. Compared to what happens to you we'll barely have a scratch. You'll also lose most or all of your nuclear capability and you still have Russia to deal with – and they're a lot closer than we are. Taking Pantex would have been a major coup, enlarging your nuclear capability by several orders of magnitude... but you didn't take Pantex did you? We can launch hundreds of nukes and not even touch our reserve."

But you said you were bored with this, so I'll also finish fast. You have twelve hours to begin a total withdrawal of all land and Naval forces. We'll clean them up anyway if you don't. But every good turn deserves another, so you have twelve hours to begin withdrawing all troops and your Navy. And let's say two weeks to get your men off our land and one more day to see your Navy steam home at maximum speed. Twelve hours or I launch."

The smooth voice came back over the radio without hesitation, "Ha ha ha Adrian. I feel like I'm in one of your western movies, standing in the street bracing another gun fighter. Very entertaining. But your gun is unloaded, and mine isn't. Coming from a – how shall we say it, lower background? – You may not be aware that your ICBMs are designed to navigate off of satellite signals, and of course the satellites are all dead. We, on the other hand, have redesigned our missile's navigation systems so that they do not need satellites. But, go ahead and pull the trigger if it makes you feel better. It'll be amusing to watch your hammer fall on an empty cylinder."

Adrian replied, "Aw, Xao, you seriously think we didn't figure that out? We retrofitted ours for astral navigation a long time ago. Like the trebuchet, it's old-school, but it still works. A small margin of error doesn't matter in this game, and our margin of error is tried and true... and small. Twelve hours, Xao, twelve hours or look up into the skies."

Adrian flipped off the connection.

"Jesus Christ, sir! Do we really have all of the missiles retrofitted?" Morgan almost shouted.

"Most of them," Adrian said with a shrug. "More than enough. We started the first week I had control of the military. My father had been in the Air Force and told me about those old navigation systems. Now, get out orders to evacuate as many people as you can from here and every other potential target, including Fort Brazos; they're sure to try and hit it. Twelve hours isn't much, but it may be all we have."

"You really think they'll launch, then?"

"There is no mathematical certainty where human actions are concerned. It hinges on whether he believes me about the navigation system... or not. In either case, this is the only action to take. Call his bluff. Part of what I said about targets is true. We have few, they have many. But they can do more damage to us than we can stand. If he believes we can hit him, he'll withdraw; he has too much to lose, and a closer problem to deal with in Russia."

Adrian glanced up Morgan. "We'll know soon enough, won't we?"

CHAPTER 23

"**M**ISSILES ARE READY TO LAUNCH when you give us the green light sir." Morgan reported. "Evacuations?"

"The word is out and people are leaving the target cities; but it's only been three hours, so it won't be many at this point, sir."

"Fort Brazos?"

"I hear it's emptying out rapidly. They're an organized community and understand the importance of the target, sir."

"Good. How's the mutiny going?"

"Tense sir, it's very tense."

"Would it be a good idea for me to address them?"

"An excellent idea, sir, the com is ready to go. Just pick up the microphone and talk, sir."

Adrian gave the Captain a tight grin, acknowledging his preparations. "Ah, a perfect XO, always one step ahead of the Captain. Okay then...

"If I could have your attention for a few moments?" Adrian spoke into the microphone. "First I want to play a recording of my conversation with the Chinese Emperor; afterwards, I'll have a few words to say."

Adrian looked at Morgan with one eyebrow raised. Morgan leaned over and flipped a switch and the recording went over the ships speakers.

Adrian nodded at Morgan with another smile of acknowledgement.

Morgan flipped the switch back when the recording ended and pointed at the microphone to signify that it was live again. Adrian picked it up.

Although the hands in the com room remained studiously attentive to their chores Adrian could hear faint sounds of cheering through the open bulkhead hatch. He waited to let it settle down then said, "That was for full disclosure; you now know everything I know – except I wasn't bluffing. Most of our missiles *have* been retrofitted. If we launch, we will completely destroy China."

Adrian again paused to allow the new wave of cheering to settle. "And we will take the hits they can certainly deliver. As you are well aware, Corpus Christi is a high-priority target. We will not survive if they launch. Essential personnel will have to stay, but only them. The rest of you have been given your orders to evacuate and it disturbs me deeply that you have mutinied by failing to follow orders and remained on board. Be that as it may, you still have time to clear the area and to receive a presidential pardon for the mutiny. Transport is ready and can get you out of the kill zone. Understand this, *I do not know if they will launch or not. If they do, you will die.* If you leave you'll leave with a sense of guilt... I get that. Your deaths will accomplish nothing, but your lives will. This country needs you to rebuild it, especially if we get nuked. It does not need you to die. So this is an order. Directly from me to each and every one of you. *Get off this ship and get as far away as you can.* I am ordering every person off this ship except Captain Morgan and myself. I would order him, too, but he would refuse on the tradition that you all know so well. So I won't order him. All I have to do now is operate this microphone, and if for some reason I can't, there's a solid backup plan in place. Your singular efforts have been critical up to this point. Now they're not. So please get off the ship and out of danger, right now. That's not a request, it's an order. Thank you."

There was no cheering this time, only silence.

Adrian hung up the radio, almost sadly.

Morgan whispered, "Thank you Mr. President. Thank you very much for saving my crew, and not dishonoring me with an order to abandon my ship, sir."

"I'd go out to shake their hands as they depart, but it would only slow them down, wouldn't it?"

"Yes sir it would, and I dare say if they saw you in person right now they'd refuse to leave again. It's bad enough to have one mutiny on my shoulders, two I don't think I could stand... as much as I agree with them. Sir, I can't tell you how proud of them I am for refusing to abandon ship. I've never been prouder, sir, never. It's the best mutiny I ever heard of. But they have to go, and God willing we'll be here for them to come back to."

"Six hours, Captain. Amazing that we've come to be in this time and place isn't it? The series of little accidents that slightly deflected our lives, putting us on new paths, thousands of little twists and turns that led us up to this. One less deflection – or maybe one more deflection – and we'd not be here. Little things like catching a red light could cause a cascade of consequences making little tiny changes that ripple down our lifetimes. Instead of here I could have been in a thousand different places, even dead. Yet here we are."

"Sir, there's still enough time for you to evacuate. I can stay and report in until the end, if that helps. "

"Morgan, that's possibly the best offer I've never heard. Your offer of sacrifice leaves me *almost* speechless. But, like the town marshal in the old movie *High Noon*, I just can't. It is not possible."

"No, sir, I didn't think so, sir, but I had to try at least once, sir. Duty demands it."

"Well said Morgan."

They returned to patiently watching the clock. Eyes focused on the second hand as the clock arms inexorably advanced, silently ticking off the seconds. There was nothing else to watch, nothing else to say, nothing to do but wait.

At two minutes before the eleventh hour the radio crackled and the Admiral said, "Chinese Naval fleets are withdrawing Mr. President – rapidly. And the entirety of the invasion forces have halted in their tracks. Two have already reversed course."

"Thank you Admiral. Doesn't mean they won't, launch though. Give the Chinese safe passage along the most direct routes back to their ships. If they stray from the direct path, have them reminded, will you? And keep me informed?"

The Admiral replied. "Absolutely, sir."

Morgan said, "You think they might still launch sir?"

"No, not really. But best to play this one safe. Put out the order for everyone to stay away from the targets for the next twenty-four hours. After that they may as well go home."

Twenty-four hours later, Adrian shook the hand of every returning sailor and Marine. Then he flew, what he hoped was his last flight for a long time, home to Linda and yet another hero's welcome home.

Eventually, he hoped, he would get used to the public spectacle of welcome wherever he went, but probably not for a long time.

Six months later.

Adrian offered a handful of corn to one of the horses in the corral. Linda standing next to him, scrutinizing his face. "It's been six months, Adrian, and you still look haunted. Your hair turning white is understandable – you went through horrific conditions, making decisions for millions of people, maybe a billion lives were in your hand, both American and Chinese. But you made the right choices. You did the right things, hard things. The Admiral's death was another blow, I know you really admired and loved that man and so did I. He went out a victor and on his own ship. He wouldn't have wanted any more than that darling. The war's over, and you won it. The Coalition of Sovereign States is gaining new members every week. Even Canadian and Mexican States are joining in.

"Each State a sovereign of its own, with a Constitution like the one created here in Texas. Decentralization is the word of the decade. Small governments that belong to a large mutual defense and trade coalition. People are freer, have more liberty than ever. Even more than in 1776 or 1865. Governments are taking shape in a way to avoid excesses of power, yet be strong enough to hold everything together. It's unbeatable in more ways than I can express. And it's all because of you, dear. The people know it, that's why you're the President not of just the Republic of Texas, but the Coalition of Sovereign States."

Adrian began to speak but stopped when Linda put her finger across his lips. "Hush for a moment darling. You're just going to protest, but let me speak. Allow me to finish. I need to say this. History thrust you into the right time and the right place so many times that it defies your belief – and it's true you had that greatness thrust upon you, you weren't born to it, didn't want it, still don't want it. But it was *you* that responded to that thrust, though reluctantly. It was *you* that responded with the strength of will and character that make people want to follow you... to the death if necessary, and many of them did die. That's what weighs on you, that they followed you and that so many died because of it.

"I know that you already know the bigger picture, the reasons they died for, it's why you made the hard decisions you made. And knowing that still doesn't assuage that inner guilt, that small voice that maybe you could have done it better and saved more lives. Or that maybe someone else would have done better if only you had let them. Those self-doubts are part of what makes you a great leader... a great man... because it shows you truly care. And even knowing that can't help you. And that, too, is part of what makes you great, and loved by so many. Because you always want to do better, and you always will want to do better, and you will always think you could've done better...it's your ingrained character."

Again Adrian started to speak and again Linda shushed him.

"I can only think of one thing that will help, something else for you to focus on." Taking Adrian's hand she placed it on her stomach and said, "And this will be just the first of many darling, just the first."

EPILOGUE

April 3, Mid-Morning, Two Years Previous

URING THE NIGHT, THE EFFECTS of the chemical had slowly begun to wear off. Adrian hadn't realized it was diminishing. He slept, unaware that his eye had closed. He had vivid dreams of a strange future. It was the last time he would dream of it.

Adrian awoke and was immediately overwhelmed by disorientation. He had fallen asleep in the woods near Fort Brazos, but had awakened in what he could only describe as a dimly lit laboratory.

A voice began speaking. Adrian focused and watched the speaker as he spoke. "Welcome to the future Adrian. You'll be experiencing a wild swing of disorientation that will last a few days, slowly diminishing as this new reality you find yourself in actually becomes real for you, because my friend, it is real. We have snatched you over a thousand years into the future. It's mind-bending for you, but you'll soon enough discover it's not only real, but it's utterly necessary."

Adrian grunted and rolled off the platform he was lying on and stood up. Physically he felt fine; better in fact than he had in a long time. "Strange dream

I'm having here," he said, talking to himself and not the tall, somewhat emaciated, white-haired man who had moved to stand in front of him.

The stranger replied. "Good. Perfect reaction. Just what I wanted to see. It could have gone two other ways – hysterics or immediate acceptance. Neither of those would have been optimal. Now, before you have a chance to formulate questions, let me tell you a little about the situation you find yourself in."

Adrian studied the man's face closely and found nothing threatening or offensive about it.

"As I said, over a thousand years have passed since your 'time' as it were. This world is radically different than yours was. And yet, it is formatted primarily on tenets you put in place during your political career. Self-reliance and decentralization to be a bit more specific. In today's world everyone provides their own food and energy, although in highly technological ways. There are no cities, no highways, no bureaucracies, no governments. Everyone lives on their own... farm... let's call it. We've learned to modify the weather, and eliminated crime and war. In fact, even the genetic structure of humans in this time is vastly different than yours. Over the centuries since your time, technology bloomed again, but in ways you wouldn't recognize. I won't need to explain shortly, we'll be giving you all that knowledge in an injection.

"We disagreed at first whether we should give you the knowledge before you awoke or not. Eventually I was able to prevail on humanitarian grounds. My suggestion, and the one that carried the day, is that you should awake in your natural state of mind, be given an opportunity to acclimate for a bit, and then have the option of allowing us to infuse the knowledge, or not, depending on your decision. My most heartfelt desire is that you volunteer, and there is a truly compelling reason for that. But, we'll get to that reason later. Too soon for that now. Oh, manners! I completely forgot. I am Dr. Hunter. I am your direct descendant – you are my Great Grandfather to several powers. I can't tell you how thrilling this is for me."

Adrian sat down on the platform and continued to stare at the stranger. 'Confused' didn't begin to cover it. This was an extremely vivid dream, no doubt. Adrian considered that his best response at this point was silence. Then he reconsidered.

"Okay, Dr. Hunter. Let's just pretend this isn't a dream or a hallucination. How in the hell will you be able to convince me that it's real? "

"Oh that's fairly easy to answer: duration. Dreams and hallucinations have short lives. As time progresses you'll slowly become centered again and will realize this is reality. We've had some small experience with this, but very little. Messing around with time is extraordinarily dangerous, and we stopped doing it almost immediately, centuries ago, shortly after we learned how and began to recognize the implications. You must understand that, in this instance, we felt there was no choice. But... well never mind, that will all become clear in due course."

Adrian pondered this for a long minute. "Okay then explain this. Language evolves rapidly. There's no way you can speak in my 'time's' colloquial. Even though a form of English may still be spoken a thousand years in the future, it would sound completely bizarre to me – and you don't."

"That's brilliant, Grandfather. And would be entirely true, except... how do I explain this...? We can inject any kind of knowledge. We can inject you with the complete, up-to-date, state-of-the-art knowledge of say... what you used to call 'quantum physics,' and within seconds you would have that knowledge at your fingertips. Languages are easy by comparison."

"Don't call me 'Grandfather.' I don't even have children. Yet." Adrian shook his head. "This is really messed up," he said to himself.

"Sorry, Adrian. I'm afraid I presumed. Would you like to go outside for a walk?"

"Explain this to me then," Adrian said, ignoring the question. "How do you control the weather?"

"Ah, another excellent question! You most certainly have an exceptional mind, picking that out as a way of confirming this isn't reality. Well it turns out that was quite easy. In layman's terms, then. The sun is a relatively steady state energy generator. Together with the Earth's tilted axis and a few other random factors, it's the sun's influence that creates weather patterns. Heat from the sun is not uniformly distributed across the earth – we evened those differences out. It took some time, and a great deal of trial and error, but eventually we turned the earth's weather into a pliable system.

"Basically the entire planet is now a perfect garden. There are no deserts, no tropical zones. We left the poles frozen though, the ice sheets are a necessary part of the overall system. Everywhere else it is moderate, year-round. No freezing winters, no scorching summers. Think of it as an almost continual spring, with only mild autumn so that plant life can function normally. The planet is green and lush and comfortable.

"You didn't answer my question: How?"

"Sorry, I wandered off didn't I? You seem to be better focused than I am. Fantastic! To answer the 'how' part of your question... we placed large solar screens into orbit, a huge mesh, made of what you would call nanoparticles, although far more advanced. These screens are of various sizes depending on their locations, some only a thousand miles in diameter, some much larger, strategically positioned to cool off the hottest parts of the earth's surface, or warm up entire geo-areas. Sunlight passes through the screens. Because of their composition, we can move them as needed and alter their position to block or reflect as much light as necessary. It's fairly crude technology, but then so are hammers and we still occasionally use hammers. The weather is so stable that there hasn't been a hurricane in centuries. "

Adrian stared at the Doctor. The dreamlike quality of the experience wasn't fading. "The burning question is why you brought me here. Assuming of course..."

"Yes, well. I hadn't thought we'd get to that for a couple of days. Perhaps we underestimated you, even though we thought you would adjust quicker than most. Still... I'm not sure it's time yet to talk about that."

"Then we have nothing more to talk about. Until

that's clear to me, nothing else can possibly make any sense."

The Doctor stared at Adrian, and then smiled. "You are quite something else, Grandfather. I shouldn't answer you, but you've staked a position I can't see any way of altering. So here goes. In order to eliminate crime and war, we had to go to the source of their impetus – a portion of the human genome. Aggression was once a fundamental necessity for survival and that trait became embedded through natural selection until it actually became competitive with survival of the species. So we had a choice – eliminate technology or eliminate aggression. It was a bitterly-fought battle, with the sides nearly equally drawn. But eventually we decided to eliminate aggression. It took four generations to completely eliminate the aggression genes from the gene pool at large. The world changed radically in those four generations. In place of aggression came cooperation.

"Imagine a world filled only with people cooperating with one another. Wars ceased. Crime disappeared. Soon governments ceased to exist as they were no longer necessary. We have cooperative organizations instead of governments. But, we've discovered a downside to this. We became vulnerable to aggression, because we don't have aggression to use to defend with."

Dr. Hunter paused for a moment, before continuing.

"Now here's the part you're probably going to struggle with the most. We came under attack from a non-earth intelligent species, a very aggressive one. And we lost the war with them – will lose it – overnight. That will happen in twenty-two years from the present date. So we've done the unspeakable in order to change a horrific outcome. We brought you to this time to lead us in that coming war, this second chance that time travel provides us. It's either that or accept that the human race will be eliminated by the invaders. We brought you back not only to lead us in that war, but to also use your genes to create a new warrior class. If you agree that is. If you do, then in twenty-two years you will have an army of millions of... clones."

"I'm going back to sleep," Adrian replied. "You be gone when I wake up." Adrian stretched out on the platform and closed his eyes.

"Perfectly natural reaction, Grandfather, perfectly natural."

Made in the USA
San Bernardino, CA
06 March 2014